Shelby wrenched her hand from Pete's the moment they were out of sight. She continued. "I need to protect Aunt Kay from Dan's plan—whatever it is."

"He wouldn't do anything to hurt Kay. It's just some harmless flirting." Pete pulled her close to him. "But I believe a man should make his own decisions." Then he leaned down and dropped a kiss on her lips.

"Don't do that!" She pushed him away.

"Why not? We can find out more if Dan thinks we're interested in each other."

"You can just say we are. After all, we went for a walk on the beach in the moonlight."

Pete smiled slyly. "Give me another kiss so I can tell him it was fun."

To his surprise, Shelby slid her arms around his neck and kissed him...then she bolted for the hotel lobby.

Pete shook his head. He didn't know what that was all about. But he sure liked it....

Dear Reader,

July might be a month for kicking back and spending time with family at outdoor barbecues, beach cottages and family reunions. But it's an especially busy month for the romance industry as we prepare for our annual conference. This is a time in which the romance authors gather to hone their skills at workshops, share their experiences and recognize the year's best books. Of course, to me, this month's selection in Silhouette Romance represents some of the best elements of the genre.

Cara Colter concludes her poignant A FATHER'S WISH trilogy this month with *Priceless Gifts* (#1822). Accustomed to people loving her for her beauty and wealth, the young heiress is caught off guard when her dutiful bodyguard sees beyond her facade...and gives *her* a most precious gift. Judy Christenberry never disappoints, and *The Bride's Best Man* (#1823) will delight loyal readers as a pretend dating scheme goes deliciously awry. Susan Meier continues THE CUPID CAMPAIGN with *One Man and a Baby,* (#1824) in which adversaries unite to raise a motherless child. Finally, Holly Jacobs concludes the month with *Here with Me* (#1825). A heroine who thought she craved the quiet life finds her life invaded by her suddenly meddlesome parents and a man she's never forgotten and his adorable toddler.

Be sure to return next month when Susan Meier concludes her CUPID CAMPAIGN trilogy and reader-favorite Patricia Thayer returns to the line to launch the exciting new BRIDES OF BELLA LUCIA miniseries.

Happy reading!

Ann Leslie Tuttle
Associate Senior Editor

Please address questions and book requests to:
Silhouette Reader Service
U.S.: 3010 Walden Ave., P.O. Box 1325, Buffalo, NY 14269
Canadian: P.O. Box 609, Fort Erie, Ont. L2A 5X3

The Bride's Best Man

JUDY Christenberry

SILHOUETTE *Romance*®

Published by Silhouette Books

America's Publisher of Contemporary Romance

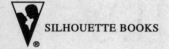 SILHOUETTE BOOKS

ISBN-13: 978-0-373-19823-8
ISBN-10:   0-373-19823-X

THE BRIDE'S BEST MAN

Visit Silhouette Books at www.eHarlequin.com

Printed in U.S.A.

Books by Judy Christenberry

Silhouette Romance

The Nine-Month Bride #1324
*Marry Me, Kate #1344
*Baby in Her Arms #1350
*A Ring for Cinderella #1356
†*Never Let You Go* #1453
†*The Borrowed Groom* #1457
†*Cherish the Boss* #1463
**Snowbound Sweetheart #1476
Newborn Daddy #1511
When the Lights Went Out… #1547
**Least Likely To Wed #1570
Daddy on the Doorstep #1654
**Beauty & the Beastly Rancher #1678
**The Last Crawford Bachelor #1715
Finding a Family #1762
††*The Texan's Reluctant Bride* #1778
††*The Texan's Tiny Dilemma* #1782
††*The Texan's Suite Romance* #1787
Honeymoon Hunt #1803
The Bride's Best Man #1823

Silhouette Books

The Coltons
The Doctor Delivers

A Colton Family Christmas
"The Diplomat's Daughter"

Lone Star Country Club
The Last Bachelor

*The Lucky Charm Sisters
†The Circle K Sisters
**From the Circle K
††Lone Star Brides

JUDY CHRISTENBERRY

has been writing romances for over fifteen years because she loves happy endings as much as her readers do. She's a bestselling author for Harlequin American Romance, but she has a long love of traditional romances and is delighted to tell a story that brings those elements to the reader. A former high school French teacher, Judy devotes her time to writing. She hopes readers have as much fun reading her stories as she does writing them. She spends her spare time reading, watching her favorite sports teams and keeping track of her two adult daughters.

Prologue

"There's a fine line between right and wrong. I hope we're coming in on the right side," Shelby Cook said, navigating through an Internet travel site. "Do you think it looks bad for us to go on a vacation so soon after we buried my mother?"

"She hasn't actually been your mother for the past ten years, honey, and you know that. Even so, you did what was necessary for her." Kay leaned back and closed her eyes, hoping to stop any further questions from her niece and soon-to-be traveling companion.

Though she was an honest person by nature, Kay Cook was participating in a deceit that she hoped would not ruin everything. She'd had this plan for some time now, and she simply had to follow her heart and head, in synch on this issue.

Shelby wasn't deterred. "I'm glad you helped me to keep a relationship with Mom. I realized she was a sad person, especially after her second marriage failed."

"You were the one bright spot in her life. That's why I encouraged her to come see you. As long as there was no man involved, she was fine."

"Is that why my father left?"

Shelby's question took her by surprise. Kay turned to face her and tried not to let the emotion show on her face. "Y-your father? You haven't ever mentioned him."

"I know. Mom always got hysterical if I asked about him when I was little." She looked down and shrugged. "It was only as I got older and saw her with a man in her life that I thought the problem might not have only been my father's, as she'd told me."

"So you wanted to meet him?"

"No, not really. After all, I've managed for most of my life without him. And, obviously, he hasn't suffered any pangs of regret or he would've contacted me."

"I see." Kay reached across her and clicked on a beachfront hotel. "Who knows? Maybe that'll change."

Chapter One

Sunshine greeted the two women as they got off the plane in Honolulu. Shelby drew a deep breath and sighed in delight as she released her pent-up breath. "Oh, this is heavenly."

Aunt Kay raised her face to the tropical sun and smiled. "See, I was right. You needed to get away from all that…that mess. Now you'll be able to relax and, if you insist, you can even study on the beach."

"Yes, you're right. After three years of law school, I needed a break." But that wasn't the only reason they'd settled on Hawaii. Her aunt Kay was there to meet the man she'd been corresponding with for fifteen years. "I bet you're excited to see your man."

"He's not mine, Shelby," she demurred. "But he is wonderful. I haven't seen him since I was a teenager, but when I told him I was coming, he offered to show us Hawaii."

"I'm sure that'll be nice," Shelby said, silently promising herself that if the man disappointed Kay, she'd make sure they only saw him once. She owed Kay that much at least.

After they reached their hotel room, Shelby suggested, "Let's get unpacked and then we can look around. And tonight we can open the lanai door and have a cool breeze sing us to sleep."

"Yes, it is so lovely here."

Not much unpacking got done before the phone rang. Her aunt snatched it up at once.

"Oh, hi, Dan. We're here."

Shelby recognized the name. Dan Jackson. Kay had told her he'd lived in her neighborhood back in Cleveland, before he'd relocated to Oahu, but the two had maintained a sweet, old-fashioned correspondence ever since. Dan's letters were the closest Kay had come to male companionship. She had seldom dated in the ten years Shelby had lived with her. Sometimes Shelby feared she was the reason. After all, she'd been only fourteen when she'd moved in with Kay, still in need of supervision.

Her mother, Cordelia, had been more interested in her own happiness than Shelby's. Even when her second husband had tried to rape Shelby, her mother had blamed Shelby for flirting with him.

Shelby had been shocked by her mother's words. She hated the man. Luckily for Shelby, her aunt had been with her mother when they discovered her fighting her stepfather. He had torn Shelby's blouse and was trying to rid her of her bra. She fought him as hard as she could, biting his hand, which earned her a slap in the face, and she screamed loudly.

Kay heard her screams and hit her brother-in-law on the head with a lamp. When Cordelia slapped Shelby, Kay insisted Cordelia leave Shelby alone. Then she told Shelby to pack her belongings. She was going home with Kay.

Shelby didn't protest. She was pleased to move to Kay's home. There she thrived, seeing a psychologist for a couple of years to be sure she recovered from the attack and her mother's rejection. Thanks to the doctor and Kay, she even learned to accept her mother as she was, as long as their visits occurred at Kay's.

After all she'd done, when Kay wanted to go to Hawaii, Shelby couldn't say no. Still, she worried about her aunt's attraction to a man she hadn't seen in a long time. Shelby was determined to protect Kay the way her aunt had once protected her.

She had always been told she was a good judge of character. She would utilize that judgment to do her best to gauge Dan Jackson's intentions toward her aunt.

From her aunt's response, she figured she'd be getting her chance tonight.

When Kay hung up the phone, Shelby asked, "So what did he say?"

"He and a friend are coming to take us out to dinner." She unpacked a couple more dresses before she looked at Shelby. "You don't mind, do you?"

Shelby was sure she'd feel like the proverbial fifth wheel, but she eagerly anticipated meeting Kay's mystery man. "No, I guess not, but I thought he'd want to have you to himself."

Kay blushed. "I told you we're just friends."

But Shelby noted her red cheeks and the way she avoided looking at Shelby. With her aunt, they were sure signs she wasn't being honest. Aunt Kay was easy to read. Shelby hoped Dan was just as obvious.

"What are you going to wear?"

Shelby's head snapped up. "Me? I would think what you're wearing is more important."

"I want you to look nice. Wear your new sundress, okay?"

Shelby had resisted the urge to buy a new wardrobe, as Kay had suggested. But she'd acquiesced on one new sundress. In fact, they'd each bought a dress that showed up their particular charms. Shelby, with her auburn hair, had a green print, and Kay, her beautiful face framed by soft blond hair, had a blue print.

"I'll wear mine if you'll wear yours," she suggested.

"It's a deal!" Kay agreed with enthusiasm. "We'll knock them dead!"

Such effusiveness from her normally calm and quiet aunt surprised Shelby. Concerned her, too.

Was Kay in love with this man? And why was Shelby so afraid of that? She wanted her aunt to have some happiness. She was only thirty-four, ten years older than Shelby. Certainly young enough to find love, have a family.

But with a man who'd written her for fifteen years without making an effort to see her?

Shelby's inner sensors went on alert. Something was screwy.

When they were both dressed in their new sundresses, makeup on and hair fixed, they descended to the lobby. Shelby had braided her long hair, even though Kay wanted her to leave it loose, on her shoulders.

"We're early. Want to go look in that shop? They have some pretty dresses," Kay said. She loved shopping.

"No, I don't think so. You go ahead, though."

"Dan is tall with dark hair. Call me if you think you see him."

"You don't have a picture of him?"

"No, I don't."

"Then maybe I can pick up more than one tall, dark-haired man, so you'll have a choice," Shelby said with a grin.

Kay looked shocked. "Oh! I...I don't think I should go look."

"I was teasing. You've got plenty of time before he arrives."

Though Kay appeared uneasy, she moved to the dress shop, but she kept her gaze fixed on Shelby.

Shelby felt bad. Her teasing had upset Kay and spoiled her shopping. She relaxed in the chair she'd chosen and watched people enter the lobby.

A few minutes later a pair of men entered. Both

were tall and handsome, but one was considerably older than the other. Too old for Kay.

Shelby stiffened as she noticed the older man staring at each person in the lobby. Could this be Dan? She got up and moved toward the shop to check with Kay.

Her aunt turned when Shelby called her name. She didn't have to ask about the man because when Kay's gaze moved past Shelby, her face lit up. She ran and hugged the man Shelby had wondered about.

"Dan! I'm so happy to see you!"

Dan replied in kind, then kissed Kay on the cheek. In Shelby's judgment, Dan seemed a bit more intense than an old friend.

Then his gaze shifted to Shelby. Much to her surprise, he stepped closer, as if he was going to hug her, too. But she immediately held out her hand, stopping him in midstep.

"How do you do?" she said stiffly.

He took her hand with a rueful grin. "I'm fine. Sorry, but I knew you when you were very little. I'm pleased to say you're just as pretty today as you were a little over twenty years ago."

"I'm sorry. I don't remember you."

"Not a problem." He turned toward his dark-haired, brown-eyed companion. "Allow me to introduce Peter Campbell, a friend of mine and an officer in my company."

Shelby nodded but said nothing.

Dan continued the introductions. "Pete, this is Shelby Cook, Kay's niece. And, of course, this is Kay Cook."

Shelby knew she hadn't been gracious, but Pete barely returned her nod. He did, however, take Kay's hand and kiss it with a big smile on his face. Was Pete the one Kay was interested in? Shelby estimated his age to be around thirty, a little younger than Kay. Still, Pete would be better for Kay than Dan who, with graying at the temples, looked about fifty.

"Shall we go, ladies?" Dan asked.

Shelby wanted to say no. For some reason she wanted to hurry to the airport and get out of Hawaii in spite of the lovely sunshine and gentle breezes.

Kay, on the other hand, happily took Dan's arm and sailed out of the hotel.

"Miss Cook?"

Shelby looked at the younger man who'd called her. He was offering her his arm, as Dan had done to Kay, albeit more reluctantly. She moved forward, but she didn't take his arm.

Dan and Kay weren't walking fast, so they caught up with them quickly.

"Where are we going?" Shelby asked.

"To the hotel next door. Its restaurant is known worldwide," Dan answered. The man beside Shelby said nothing.

Shelby was wearing flats because she was five-nine, so walking to another hotel wasn't a problem. Kay, though, had on high heels. Maybe it was good that she was clinging to Dan's arm. Shelby supposed she wore heels because she knew Dan was so tall.

Pete was tall, also, which was nice for Shelby. She

didn't go out with short men. Of course, she seldom went out at all, so it wasn't difficult to eliminate one segment of the male population.

Neither, she reminded herself, was she going out with Pete. He was simply tagging along with Dan, as she was with Kay.

In the restaurant, the maître d' asked if they wanted to dine on the beach or in the dining room.

"On the beach? We can do that?" Kay asked.

Dan smiled. "I believe the lady has chosen."

"Very well, sir. If you'll follow me?"

Shelby wouldn't deny Kay's desire to eat on the beach, so she didn't voice her doubts about an enjoyable dinner. Of course, she had doubts about the dinner for other reasons, too.

Once she stepped outside, however, she had to admit dining on the beach was a wonderful choice. Their table for four was set on a silken tarp, with the long tablecloth fluttering in the ocean breeze. Once they were seated, Shelby looked up and saw a moon rising in the sky over Pete's shoulder.

"Look, Kay. Do you see the moon?" Shelby asked, gesturing toward Pete.

Pete looked at Shelby. "You don't call her Aunt Kay?"

Shelby stared at the man before saying briefly, "No, not always. She's only ten years older than me."

"Really?" Pete asked, staring at Kay.

"Yes, really," Shelby returned. She didn't like the way the man was looking at Kay, as if sizing her up.

"Most people think I'm her mother," Kay said with a chuckle.

"You are more my mother than my real mother ever was," Shelby said softly, taking Kay's hand.

Dan took her other hand. "She's right, Kay, and we all know it."

Shelby looked at Dan. "How do you know?"

"Kay wrote me about what happened."

"You knew my mother?"

"We met," he said briefly, shrugging his shoulders.

"And my father? Did you know him?"

"About as much as I knew your mother. I was more Kay's friend."

"So why did you move to Hawaii?" Shelby asked.

"I was in a bad situation and I needed to get away."

Since Kay would've been only in her midteens, Shelby guessed she couldn't blame him for leaving. "What does your company do, Dan?"

"Oh, a mixture of things. I import cars and sporting equipment, and I export Hawaiian items, such as macadamia nuts, leis, muumuus, most anything we think will sell on the mainland."

"How interesting." Shelby looked at Kay, to see if what he did was a surprise to her.

"Doesn't that sound exciting, Shelby?" Kay asked.

"Yes, exciting," Shelby agreed.

"What do you do, Shelby?" Dan asked.

"I just finished law school." With a bright smile, she added, "But I guess you and Kay have more in common."

Dan and Kay smiled at each other.

Pete needed more details. "Why do you say that?"

"They're both in retail."

Pete looked at Kay. "What do you sell?"

"Oh, I have a secondhand furniture store," Kay said in a deprecating manner.

"Really," Pete said. "Maybe we should start one of those here on the island. It certainly wouldn't be worth shipping anything back to the mainland."

Dan frowned. "I don't know much about furniture, but it does sound like a good idea."

"Maybe I should look into it. I'll make some calls tomorrow and do some research to see if there are secondhand stores on the island."

"Good idea, Pete. I bet Kay could give you advice."

"Would you mind, Kay?" Pete asked.

"I would enjoy it."

"And I'll take you to lunch, Shelby, so you won't feel left out," Dan said with an easy smile.

"That's quite all right. I'll be fine lying at the pool and studying. I've planned to do that, but I was worried about Kay being entertained. That will work out just fine."

Kay protested. "But, Shelby—"

"You promised me I could study if I felt the urge, Kay, and I do." She gave her aunt a serious look.

"I know I did, but I was hoping you wouldn't want to."

It was Dan who eased the situation. "Don't worry about it, Kay. Let Shelby study all day. Then, tomorrow night, we'll all four go out to dinner."

"But, Dan, you bought dinner tonight. I can't let you take us out again."

"Actually, he hasn't paid for dinner tonight yet," Shelby said. "Maybe it would be better if we split the cost tonight." Shelby caught the look of outrage on Pete's face. Dan didn't seem upset at all.

"Nice try, young lady," Dan said with a chuckle, "but I extended the invitation, so I'll pay the bill."

"Then you'd better save your money tomorrow night."

"Shelby!" Kay said in an admonishing tone. "There's no need to insult Dan. He's been a wonderful host."

"I didn't mean to insult him. But I don't know him. If he wants to take you out, he shouldn't feel he has to drag me along. You're old enough. You don't need a chaperone."

Dan laughed. "You're a straight shooter, aren't you, Shelby?"

"I try to be."

"Okay, we'll negotiate. I feel I owe Kay another dinner if she works all day with Pete tomorrow. But my chances of repaying Kay while abandoning you are nil. You know her. Am I right?"

"Yes, Dan, you're right. I didn't know if you knew Kay that well."

"Even when she was young, she kept her dolls all together because she didn't want any of them to think she was the favorite."

Kay blushed and looked away from the table.

"Kay! You never told me that!"

"That wasn't anything you needed to know," her aunt said sheepishly.

Dan smiled at her. "Sorry to spill the beans on you, sweetheart. But it was something that had stuck in my memory."

Shelby was beginning to see why Kay had remembered him for so long.

Kay managed to change the subject back to Pete's original suggestion. Shelby allowed the three-sided conversation to flow for the rest of dinner without interruption. When they'd finished their meal, Dan leaned over and whispered something in Kay's ear. Shelby noticed Pete's complete attention was on Kay's face.

"Oh, I'd love to," Kay exclaimed.

Dan looked at Shelby. "I suggested to Kay that we take off our shoes and walk back to your hotel along the beach, instead of the way we came."

Shelby frowned, unsure what her answer should be. What did Kay want her to do?

"Oh, Shelby, let's! We can even wade a little bit. That would be heavenly," Kay enthused.

"Of course, if that's what you want."

"Good!" Kay jumped up from her chair and stepped out of one shoe, then the other. Shelby did the same.

"You might as well sit down, ladies. Our shoes don't come off as easily as yours," Dan said with a smile.

"Oh, I'm sorry!" Kay apologized. "I'm just so excited!"

"I don't mind your excitement. It makes me feel young again."

"You *are* young, Dan," Kay said.

Dan grinned and shook his head. "Maybe you need

your eyesight checked, sweetheart." Then he stood with his shoes in one hand and offered his other hand to Kay. "Ready to go?"

"Oh, yes!" Kay exclaimed, seizing his hand.

Before Shelby could even think of moving, they were walking along the beach.

"I'm sorry," she apologized to Pete. "I didn't mean to hold you up."

"Are you sure about that?"

Shelby stared at the young man. "I beg your pardon?"

"I haven't been able to decide if you approve of Dan for Kay. You want to clue me in?"

Shelby gave him a look. "And I was trying to decide if you wanted Kay for Dan or for yourself! Want to clue *me* in?" she said, echoing his words.

"Lady, I don't want to tell you anything!"

"Same here!"

With each retort they stepped closer to each other, until they were a foot apart. When she realized it, Shelby turned away, giving him her back in a wordless gesture that spoke volumes.

Neither said anything for a few moments, until Pete broke the icy silence. "Come on. We're losing sight of them."

He didn't bother offering his hand, which was good because Shelby wouldn't have accepted anything from him.

Chapter Two

Shelby and Pete marched down the beach as if they had no knowledge of the other's presence. Dan and Kay, on the other hand, drifted along the beach, hands linked, through the waves.

After the men had bade them good-night, the two ladies rode the elevator to their floor in silence. But as they entered their room, Kay exclaimed, "Wasn't that a wonderful evening?"

"I assume that's a rhetorical question," Shelby said.

Kay came to an abrupt halt and stared at her niece. "You didn't have a good time?"

"Dinner on the beach was nice. That certainly doesn't happen in Cleveland." Shelby avoided any comment about the men.

"Yes, that was lovely, wasn't it?" Kay sat down on her bed. "What did you think of Dan?"

"He's quite charming."

"Yes, he always has been." She had a faraway look in her eyes. "It almost seems like yesterday that I'd seen him."

Unable to hold back any longer, Shelby blurted, "He must be twenty years older than you, Kay!" She hadn't meant to say anything negative, but she couldn't help it.

"No, he's not! Dan is only twelve years older than me."

"And you've been writing for fifteen years?"

"Well, that's when it first began, but we didn't write much until after I moved out of Cordelia's house."

"Mom didn't approve?"

The dreamy look fled Kay's face. "No," she said in a clipped tone.

"Why?"

"It doesn't matter. I'm going to bed. I think the time change is catching up with me."

She found her nightgown and went into the bathroom, leaving Shelby sitting on her bed. She crossed her arms over her chest. So her mother hadn't approved of Dan? That was interesting. Her mother hadn't had high standards, so what had he done? Robbed a bank?

She opened the sliding door and walked out on the lanai. The gentle breeze and lapping waves distracted her from her thoughts for a minute. Then her mind returned to the contemplation of Kay and Dan Jackson.

The man was charming, as she'd said, but not so

charming that he sounded like a snake oil salesman. He appeared intelligent and patient. Certainly more than her. Impatience was one of her biggest faults. Darn it, the only thing she could find wrong with Dan was his age.

"I'm out of the bath, Shelby," Kay called out.

When Shelby didn't come in at once, Kay came closer to the lanai. "Aren't you tired?"

"Yes, I suppose so." Shelby moved back into the room. "Is it okay if I leave the door open a little so we can hear the waves?"

"Oh, yes, I think that's a very relaxing sound."

"Me, too."

After they were both in bed, Shelby intended to question Kay about her relationship with Dan. But she discovered her aunt Kay was already asleep. Apparently nothing was bothering her conscience. And nothing should. She was a wonderful person, in spite of the tragedies that had surrounded her life.

Kay's parents had died in a car crash when she was ten. That was when she'd moved into Cordelia's home. Shelby had been born that same year. Cordelia had turned Kay into a babysitter at once. Though Shelby had vague memories of her father's presence, she didn't remember much about him. But Kay's presence in her life was clear. Together they went through the trauma of Cordelia's divorce and the ensuing years. Shelby remembered her mother's hysterics before every one of her father's visits. Now she could admire his courage, but it hadn't lasted long. The visits soon stopped.

She remembered being upset when she didn't see him again, when she couldn't picture him in her mind. But as she listened to her mother describe him in mean, hateful words, soon it became easier to forget him. Cordelia loathed him so intensely, she had Shelby's name changed back to her maiden name, Cook. It was as if all memory of her father had been erased.

Then, after her mother remarried, Shelby learned men were untrustworthy. It was a life lesson she'd rather forget but would always remember.

Banishing the memories, she listened to the waves and let them rock her to sleep.

Morning had barely dawned when Shelby awoke. A peek at the bedside clock told her it was only six-thirty, but the time change was wreaking its usual havoc.

"Guess you haven't adapted to the time zone, either." Apparently Kay was awake, too.

Shelby got out of bed. "I'll probably fall asleep right after lunch." Then she noticed her aunt was already dressed, in a blue pantsuit. "You're on the go already?"

"You remember, I'm going to do some work with Pete today," Kay explained, looking all too happy, in Shelby's opinion. When she made a face, her aunt sobered. "You're okay with that, aren't you? I mean, you're not…jealous, are you?"

Shelby stopped her hairbrush midstroke. What reason would she have to be jealous of her aunt spending the day with Pete Campbell? Actually, she was counting her lucky stars that she got out of joining them. She continued brushing her hair and affected a light tone. "Why would I be jealous?"

"Well, Pete was your…escort last night."

"If you want him, Aunt Kay, you can have him."

Her aunt came up behind her at the dresser mirror. "You're not interested in him? I mean, he is handsome. And successful and charming and—"

Shelby turned around to silence Kay. "I'm not interested in Pete or any man right now."

"But you're finished with school. It's no longer an excuse for you to ignore men."

"I haven't ignored them. I just haven't had time for them."

Before Kay could argue, she was interrupted by a rap on the door and a male voice calling, "Room service." She turned to Shelby. "I hope you don't mind, but I ordered us breakfast. I thought we could eat on the lanai." She went to the door and directed the waiter where to set the tray.

When they were sitting on the lanai enjoying the fresh island pineapple, Kay let out a sigh. "Oh, this is so nice."

Shelby gave her a smile. "Now that I won't argue with."

Kay, not to be deterred, asked, "Are you sure you don't want to go with us today?"

"I'm sure. I'm going to sit at the pool and study, and maybe take a walk on the famous Waikiki Beach. A nice, relaxing day."

"But you'll be back for dinner, right? You remember our plans."

Shelby set down her juice, not saying anything.

What she wouldn't give to get out of that little soiree tonight. She looked up at her aunt, at the expectant look on her face, and couldn't back out. "Yes, Kay, I'll be ready."

After all, she reasoned, she didn't want to leave her aunt alone with Dan until she could figure out what he was up to. And what her aunt was up to, she added. For a moment there Kay seemed almost too intent on Shelby joining them, as if there was a special reason. Could Kay have an ulterior motive?

Aunt Kay? An inner voice questioned. If ever there was an honest person who didn't know guile, it was Kay Cook.

No, Shelby told herself. If there was something going on, it was on Dan's part. And tonight she'd do her best to find out what.

After a peaceful, solitary afternoon, Shelby took a taxi to Dan's office. He'd called to offer her a ride to dinner, but she'd insisted on meeting him at Island Traders.

She looked at her watch and realized she'd be a little early, but she decided to go ahead to Dan's offices.

Maybe Kay and Pete would already be there. Shelby had worked in Kay's store frequently as she'd grown up. She was eager to hear what they had found today.

She enjoyed the solitary ride in the back of the taxi. Hawaii was an incredible state, so different from the others she'd visited. When the taxi stopped in front of a three-story white stucco building surrounded by palm trees and colorful hibiscus, she paid the driver and walked in.

She made her way up to the third floor, where, according to the lobby directory, Dan's company was located. About to open the door to Suite 300, she heard Pete's voice.

"Why did you invite *her?*"

"Because Kay wants her here. What's the problem? You said you didn't mind helping me out." That was Dan's voice.

"I just don't see the need for her. She's stiff and unfriendly."

"But she's pretty," Dan said.

"I'm not interested!" Pete protested.

"Careful, or you're going to ruin my plan."

Plan? Shelby immediately wondered what his plan was. Could Dan have an investment he was trying to sell Aunt Kay? Did he want to steal her money?

Before she could think further, Pete said, "I'd better go down if I'm going to pay her taxi when it arrives."

Panicked, Shelby turned and ran down the hall as the door opened.

She hadn't escaped unnoticed because Pete hollered, "Shelby, wait!"

She didn't. When she reached the elevator, she jabbed the button, but the door didn't open, so she chose the stairs. Glad her sandals were flat, she hurried down the two flights of stairs.

When she opened the door on the ground floor, she found Pete leaning against the wall beside it.

"Whoa! Shelby, stop running." He caught her arm to ensure she did as he ordered.

"Let me go!"

"Why? You're supposed to join us for dinner."

She glared at him. "I've changed my mind!"

"Why?"

Shelby tried to twist her arm free of his hold, but he wouldn't allow it. "Because I don't like the idea of Dan's plan!"

Pete studied the young woman he was holding. Last night he hadn't been at all attracted. Her sharp tongue had cut him with one too many sassy retorts. At times she'd been aloof, at others, downright surly, and always uninterested. In everything except Dan.

Today, though, her blue eyes flared to life, her red locks flamed in the sunshine pouring through the lobby doors. She looked like another person. A very attractive person.

Last night he'd had a name for her. Not one he could repeat in mixed company. Right now he was tempted to call her a looker.

He felt a tug deep within him, both surprised and de-lighted at the same time. Relishing the feel of her, he had to force his concentration onto the topic at hand.

"You know what Dan's plan is?" he asked in surprise.

"Don't you?"

"No, Dan didn't explain it to me."

"I don't believe you. You're helping him, aren't you?" Shelby demanded. "Why would you do that if you don't know what the plan is?"

Why? Because Dan Jackson had saved him once upon a time. Pete feared thinking what he'd be, where he'd be, if he hadn't been lucky enough to meet Dan. Raised on Oahu by a single mother who worked two jobs, Pete had no family around him. Dan had become his family, especially when his mother died while Pete was in college.

He looked Shelby right in the eye and said, "Because Dan is more than my boss. He's my best friend. Because Dan became my Big Brother when I was a teenager, replacing my father, whom I hadn't seen since I was a little boy. Because Dan kept me from going down the wrong road and showed me the right way. Because I trust him."

"Even if what he wants involves spending the evening with a stiff, unfriendly, unattractive woman?" Shelby asked. So apparently she'd overheard part of his conversation with Dan back in the office. He'd hoped not.

He shot her a grin. "Even if." Then he began walking toward the elevator, pulling her with him.

She yanked on her arm again. "Let me go. You couldn't pay me to have dinner with you, or Dan!"

He stopped and she looked at him expectantly. "Do you want to disappoint Kay? She's spent all day talking about you."

"Oh, that's what's wrong. She bored you to death today."

"No, she didn't. Now, come on, let's go join them."

"Where is Kay? She wasn't in the office."

"She excused herself to freshen up." He gazed down at her, thinking how good she looked, like a spitfire, with her eyes squinting at him in suspicion. His voice lowered and he stepped a bit closer. "Come on, Shelby. You can convince me my description was off base."

She seemed taken aback, but held her ground. "I'll do no such thing!"

"So you *are* stiff, unfriendly and unattractive?" He smiled at her.

"Stop being silly!" She tried again to get loose. "I need to know what Dan's plan is."

"But I told you I don't know what his plan is."

"Will you help me find out?"

Pete stared at her. "You're asking me to betray my friend and boss? Why would I do that?" Unbelievably enough, he wanted to get on her good side, which he knew helping her would do. But how could he go against Dan?

"Because Kay is my only family. Because she took care of me and loved me when I needed it. Because she deserves to be treated fairly!" Shelby stood taller, daring him to say differently.

Pete couldn't. "I won't argue with that. And she's quite charming."

"Then you'll help me?"

"I won't do anything to hurt Dan."

"But will you help me protect Kay?"

Pete assessed her relaxed posture, how she seemed to soften right before his eyes. "You're certainly not stiff and unfriendly now, are you? And of course you were always attractive."

She ignored him. "You haven't answered my question."

"I promise I'll try to help you protect Kay, because I don't want her hurt. But I don't believe that is Dan's intention."

"All right. Then I'll go to dinner," she finally conceded.

He let his hand slide down her arm until it reached hers. He lifted it to his lips. "I salute your wisdom. Let's go. They're waiting for us," he said as he pushed the button for the elevator. This time it opened at once.

"Now it comes," Shelby muttered.

"It's all in the wrist," Pete said with a grin.

Pete watched Shelby as she answered one of Dan's questions over dinner. Now that he'd seen the fire and the loyalty in her, he saw her differently. She was gradually relaxing, becoming the woman that matched her beautiful russet hair.

"Kay, what did you think of the stores you saw today?" Shelby asked.

Kay smiled. "Well, needless to say I think my store is more organized and takes in a better quality of furniture. But the stores today seemed to be doing a remarkable business."

"Really?" Dan asked, smiling at her.

"Yes, Dan. It was quite impressive," Kay assured him. "I think I could move my business here and make a good living."

"Aunt Kay! You aren't thinking of doing that, are you?" Shelby demanded.

"Of course not! I was just thinking—"

"Why not?" Dan asked quietly.

"Because it's not home!" Shelby answered for her aunt.

"But it could be," Dan said. "Home is made up of the people you love."

Shelby had a panicky look in her eyes as she turned to Pete, as if to say, See what he's doing!

Kay finally gave her opinion. "You're right, Dan. But Shelby is like a daughter to me. I could never leave her in Cleveland and come here, no matter how beautiful Hawaii is."

"So, to get you here, I'll have to persuade Shelby to move here?" Dan asked, his voice light, as if he were teasing.

Shelby gave Pete a quick, questioning look, but he could only shrug his shoulders. He had no idea if that was Dan's plan. And truthfully tonight he didn't have much objection to it. Last night was another matter.

"I have no intention of moving to Hawaii. To pass the bar I'd have to learn an entire set of new laws. That would be too hard," Shelby told her aunt, softening her staunch words with a slight smile.

"Maybe we'll talk later," Pete said. "I might find other reasons." He wasn't surprised to see Shelby's outraged expression. But Dan drew the most interest from him. With a twinkle in his eye, his friend raised his glass in Pete's direction.

Was that it? Did he want Kay to stay? Was he in love

with her? Not that she wasn't attractive, but Dan had dated more than his share of beautiful women before.

The waiter arrived just then with their dinners and Pete didn't have to respond when Shelby whispered, "You promised!"

Maybe he could get her alone later and they could have a discussion. He wouldn't mind that. And apparently Dan wouldn't either, as he'd be left alone with Kay.

Dan offered to take them on a tour of Oahu the next day, and Kay eagerly accepted for both of them.

Pete caught Shelby's hand as she opened her mouth, no doubt to protest. He didn't want her to decline the invitation, especially since he planned to invite himself. "I'd like that, too, Dan, assuming I'm included," Pete said with a smile while he squeezed Shelby's hand.

"I—" Shelby began.

"We'll enjoy ourselves, Shelby," he hurriedly said.

"You'll come, won't you, Shelby?" Kay asked, worry in her voice.

Shelby drew a deep breath before she spoke. "Yes, of course."

Pete continued to hold her hand below the table. She hadn't pulled loose, and he saw no reason to give up the warmth of her skin against his.

As if she'd read his mind, she removed her hand from his. "What shall we go see?" she asked in a bright voice.

"Would you like to climb to the top of Diamond Head?" Dan suggested.

"Will it be too hard?" Kay asked.

"Well, it's a challenge," Dan said. "I have an idea. You and I can go by elevator up to the bar on the top floor of your hotel and wait for the other two while they climb up to the top. It has the same view."

"Wait a minute!" Pete protested. "I've already been to the top of Diamond Head. I'll join you two in the bar. Shelby can tell us all about it when she finishes the climb."

"How gentlemanly of you!" Shelby said sarcastically.

"Okay, okay," Pete teased. "We'll let you in the elevator, too."

"But that's not so exciting, going up in an elevator to look out a window," Shelby said.

Pete leaned toward Kay. "Your niece is a hard woman to please, did you know that?"

"I'm sure she doesn't mean to be," Kay said with a smile toward Shelby.

"I'll tell you what. After drinks in the bar, we can go on a dinner cruise for the sunset. How about that, Shelby?" Pete asked.

"That would be exciting."

"Is that okay with you two?" Pete asked.

Dan nodded to his friend. "It sounds good to me. How about you, Kay?"

"That sounds great. And Shelby and I can try out the beach during the day while you two work."

"Aw, spoilsport! I was hoping to see Shelby in a swimsuit," Pete said in a playful tone of voice, though he truly meant it. "Do you wear a bikini, Shelby?"

He loved her flustered look. He was seeing more sides of her tonight, and they were all beautiful.

Dan played along. "How about you, Kay?"

Kay's cheeks turned pink. "No, Dan. I'm afraid I have a one-piece suit."

"Looks like we'll have to work tomorrow, Dan," Pete said.

"Hmm, maybe half a day."

"Why only half a day?" Kay asked.

"I have my reasons," Dan teased.

To say Pete was shocked by Dan's comment was an understatement. As long as he'd known him, Dan had put in minimum twelve-hour days. Now he was taking time off for some secret reason? Maybe Shelby was right to be suspicious.

Pete owed Dan a lot. He'd worked closely with him for the past seven years and known him for thirteen years. He couldn't accept that Dan would do anything to hurt Kay.

Dinner continued, but he noted that Shelby was not as relaxed as she had been. She was back to giving one-word answers to any questions.

When the waiter offered dessert, Pete insisted they all indulge. "I want Shelby to get sweeter," he insisted.

When Shelby protested, he added, "Of course, it's really because I love chocolate. They've got a fudge brownie sundae to die for. But I'd look terrible if I ordered it and none of you had any, right?"

"Yes, you would," Shelby retorted. "But I'll sacrifice and join you because that sounds too good to pass up."

He was surprised by her words but pleased as well.

After the dessert, which they all shared, they exited the restaurant, chatting excitedly about their plans. Suddenly Shelby grabbed Pete's arms and came close to him, her mouth mere inches away from his ear. As she spoke, her warm breath on his neck stirred his fantasies. He imagined she whispered sweet nothings to him. Instead she said, "We need to talk!"

Chapter Three

When the foursome reached the hotel, Pete said, "Do you mind if Shelby and I walk on the beach for a while? It's a beautiful night."

"No, of course not," Kay said, after looking at her niece.

"We won't be long," Pete promised as he caught Shelby's hand in his and headed out the open back door to the moonlit beach.

Kay looked at Dan. "Do you suppose he's interested in her?"

"Why not? She's attractive. You don't mind, do you?"

"As long as it's nothing serious. I wouldn't want to leave her behind."

Dan studied her carefully. "You wouldn't consider moving to Hawaii?"

"I don't think I'd make a good island girl. I'm a little too old and much too serious for a carefree existence."

"I don't live a carefree existence. I run a business, but I do it here in Hawaii."

"I don't think the question will come up, Dan. These boy-girl things happen on vacations all the time."

"As I remember, when I left home, you had one of those boy-girl things going on. Whatever happened to him?"

"Tony Rico. I dumped him."

"Why?"

"Because he wanted sex, and I refused. I'd already had an example right before my eyes of a forced marriage because of a pregnancy. But that was a long time ago."

The elevator opened and Kay hurriedly said, "You don't need to see me to my room. I'm fine."

"I know you are." Dan got into the elevator anyway.

They stood silently in the elevator, surrounded by strangers. When the door opened on her floor, Kay got out, calling a good-night to Dan over her shoulder. To her surprise, he followed her down the corridor.

"Really, Dan, there's no need—"

"Yes, there is. Didn't you find anyone worth dating in the past twenty years?"

Kay backed up against her door. "I've dated occasionally, but I had Shelby to care for and…and I was happy."

"I hope so. I'd hate to think my marriage ruined four lives instead of three."

"I don't think it ruined Shelby's life. She's well adjusted and happy, too."

"Because of you." He leaned forward and dropped a kiss on her forehead. "Bless you, Kay. I'll see you to-morrow." Then he walked back to the elevator.

Kay stood there watching him until the doors closed, depriving her of the view. She reached up and touched her forehead, still warm from his kiss. Just what did he mean by that?

"What did you want to talk about?" Pete asked Shelby, who had wrenched her hand from his the moment they were out of sight.

She turned to him, her features tight. "You're treating this like it's a game! I'm serious. I want to protect Kay!"

"From what, Shelby?"

"From Dan, of course. From his plan!"

"I don't know what his plan is. But I don't believe he'd do anything to hurt Kay. All he's doing is a little flirting." Pete smiled, sure he'd erased Shelby's worries.

"You don't understand! Kay gave up her freedom to take care of me for the past ten years. I don't think she went out on more than five dates during those ten years. She's inexperienced. Flirting could hurt her a lot!"

"I promised I'd try to find out what Dan's plan is, but I can assure you he's a good man. He wouldn't hurt Kay," Pete repeated.

"But he could make Kay fall in love with him, just by flirting. That's why I need to know what he's doing. Or maybe you could tell him not to do that."

"Generally, if one works for Dan, one doesn't tell

him what to do," Pete said with a grin. "It's not good for one's health."

Her eyes narrowed. "So you're afraid of him?"

"No, I'm not." He pulled her close to him. "But I believe a man should make his own decisions." Then he leaned over and dropped a kiss on her lips.

"Don't do that!"

"Why not? I think we can find out more if Dan thinks we're interested in each other."

"You can just say we are. After all, we went for a walk on the beach in the moonlight, didn't we?"

"Well, no. We haven't actually gotten to the beach."

Shelby looked around her. They were still on the lushly landscaped grounds of the hotel. "We can see it from here."

"Well, at least give me another kiss so I can tell him the walk on the beach was fun," Pete teased.

To his surprise, Shelby, in a serious mood, leaned forward and slid her arms around his neck. He readily pulled her against him and took the kiss much deeper than the first one.

When Pete finally lifted his lips, he hungered for more, but Shelby immediately backed away, staring at him.

"I...I have to go upstairs," she said hurriedly, and rushed into the hotel lobby.

He didn't know what that was all about. But he sure liked it.

The two men were quiet for much of their drive home. Finally Dan broke the silence. "Is everything all right?"

"Yeah, sort of." Pete could think of no way to get the information from his friend other than by asking him outright. "Shelby heard you say you had a plan. She wants me to find out what it is."

Dan took his eyes off the road to look at Pete. Then he turned back to his driving. "That's my business."

"Look, Dan, I'd trust you with my life, but Shelby doesn't know you. She's afraid you're going to hurt her aunt."

"Hurt Kay? I owe her too much. Not that I'd ever even consider such a thing anyway. You can tell Shelby that Kay is safe from me."

"Then why are you flirting with her?"

Dan looked at him again, and Pete was glad they were no longer in the areas of Honolulu heavily traveled by tourists. "You're being ridiculous!"

"Am I? I noticed it as much as Shelby did. I know you're not a womanizer. So what's going on?"

"I'm showing an old friend Hawaii. That's all."

Pete tried it one more time. "So you really don't have a plan?"

"Of course not."

They finished the drive in silence.

The women didn't go to the beach until after lunch. To their surprise, the two men joined them almost at once. Dan had rented Pete and himself a room for the day so they could shower and change before they went to dinner. Driving back to their homes would take too much time.

Dan stretched out on a towel beside Kay as the other two ran into the surf together.

"How do you think your plan is working?" Kay whispered.

Dan almost choked. "My plan?"

"You know. To get to know Shelby."

He felt relieved. "I wouldn't say she's exactly taken to me. Would you?"

"No, but I think she's getting used to you."

"How about you? Are you taking to me?" he asked with a big grin.

"Oh, you!" Kay returned, smiling. "You'd better be glad I know you're teasing!"

Dan went along with her. "Right. By the way, I like your swimsuit. It looks good on you."

"Thank you. We don't do a lot of swimming in Cleveland. I'm a little white so I'm covered in sunblock."

"I'll be glad to rub some on anytime you want."

"There you go again! What with our pretending, as you suggested, you're going to have Shelby thinking the wrong thing if you don't stop that."

"Okay, I'll behave." To take his mind off her beautiful shapely legs and curved bottom, he changed the subject. "Pete told me all about your knowledge of furniture. He was quite impressed."

"I should know it. After all, I've worked in the furniture business since I was eighteen."

"I thought you started your shop after college."

"I did, using the insurance money I had from Mom and Dad's deaths. But while I was in school, I worked part-time in a furniture store. Plus, I studied furniture in college. At least, I focused on it in my interior design classes. Furniture and antiques. I did a lot of that on my own. There are books where you can look up most anything."

"Do you sometimes get antiques?"

"Yes. People don't know what they've got. Have you ever watched *The Antiques Roadshow?* They have one set in the U.S. and one in England. You can learn a lot from watching that show."

Dan raised himself on one elbow. "Did you think seriously about opening a shop here?"

She avoided his gaze. "No, of course not!"

"Why?"

Kay abruptly sat up. "Why would I? I have a perfectly good shop in Cleveland."

"Because Shelby might decide to stay in Hawaii. She wouldn't be the first person to arrive in paradise and decide not to leave."

"Like you."

It seemed like forever ago when he'd come to Oahu. Only, he'd come with every intention of staying. He'd needed to get away from Cleveland and everyone there, and Hawaii was the farthest he could go. Still, he'd fallen in love with the islands immediately.

He could tell he'd upset Kay with his questions. Before he could find a way to calm her down, she jumped to her feet.

"I think I'll cool off in the water for a few minutes."

She ran down the beach to where the waves rolled into the shore. The surf was strong today, and Dan immediately rose and followed her. He wasn't sure she'd be able to stand up if she went in too far at high tide.

She'd slowed down after she'd entered the water, feeling her way in. Shelby immediately came to her side, reaching her before Dan did.

"Aunt Kay, I'm glad you decided to come in! Isn't it great?"

Since a wave rolled over her at that moment, Kay didn't have a chance to answer. She would have gone under except for strong hands on her waist.

"I think you're in over your head, Kay," Dan whispered in her ear.

"Yes, I think I am." As soon as he let her go, she began moving back toward shore.

"Wait, Kay!" Dan called out, turning to follow her.

"What did you say to my aunt?" Shelby demanded.

"I told her I thought she was in over her head. She's shorter than all of us. I was afraid the waves would be too strong for her."

"I'll go see," Shelby said, apparently finding his words unremarkable.

"I'll go with you," Dan said.

"Hey, wait!" Pete called as he was abandoned in the ocean. With a shrug of his shoulders, he followed the others to the beach.

Kay had settled back on her towel by the time the others reached her.

"Honey, are you all right?" Dan demanded at once.

"Of course I am. There was no need for all of you to get out of the water."

"I wanted to be sure you were fine," Shelby said, studying her aunt's face.

"Yes, but I think I may go up to our room soon. I hope I haven't gotten too much of a burn. Then I wouldn't feel like going out for the dinner cruise tonight. Can you cancel the reservations if that's the case, Dan?"

"No, I've already purchased the tickets. But don't worry about it. I don't mind swallowing the cost of them if you don't feel well."

"Go on up to the room, Aunt Kay. I'll come up in a little while and see how you're doing," Shelby promised, adding, "unless you need me to go up with you."

"No, that's not necessary. But don't stay out in the sun too long. Your skin is almost as fair as mine."

"I won't, Aunt Kay."

All three of them stood on the beach and watched Kay make her way to the hotel. Then Pete spoke. "What happened?"

"I guess she had too much of the sun," Shelby said, her gaze still fixed on her aunt.

Dan met Pete's gaze and shrugged his shoulders. Anything else would be a lie. He knew now not to press Kay about Shelby moving to Hawaii.

"Maybe I should go on up," Shelby said, looking at Pete.

Dan spoke before Pete could. "No, that's not necessary. I'm going up to make some calls. I'll send something to Kay's room to rehydrate her. It'll make her feel better."

Shelby turned to look at Dan. "Okay, if you're sure."

"I'm sure. I want her to feel up to going on the cruise this evening." He started toward the hotel and then turned around. "Be sure you don't let her get too red, Pete. I'm counting on you."

Shelby slapped her hands on her hips and glared at Dan. "I think I'm capable of taking care of myself!"

"I'm sure you are in Cleveland, but the sun is deceiving here. That's all I meant, Shelby." With a wave of his hand, he strode up the beach to the hotel.

When he reached his room, he ordered a tall fruit drink and several bottles of ice water to be sent to Kay, along with a single rose in a vase and a card with his name on it. He hoped she would feel bad if she didn't come with them on the cruise and change her mind. He'd have to be more careful in the future if his plan was going to work.

The minute they were alone, Shelby whirled around. "What did Dan say about his plan?"

"He denied having one," Pete replied.

"How can he deny it? I heard it, too."

"He said something about teasing. You know how it is." Pete shrugged his shoulders and tried to catch her hand to pull her back into the water. "Let's go back in."

She held her hands behind her back. "I don't believe that. You should've pressed him."

"I tried. But he knows I trust him."

"Well, I don't. Did you say anything about flirting with Kay?"

"Yes, I did," Pete said with a sigh.

"Does that sigh mean I'm not going to like your answer?"

"Probably. He said he was just being friendly, greeting an old friend and showing her Hawaii."

She stared at him, her blue eyes wide. "Oh, poor Aunt Kay!"

"What? What's wrong?"

"Don't you see? He's been flirting with her, but he didn't mean anything by it. Now she's fallen for him and he's not interested. That must be what happened! I'm sure she's upstairs packing. We'll probably go home tomorrow."

"What? No! You can't do that!"

She gave him a frosty stare. "We certainly can if we want to!"

"But we made plans for dinner. Don't you want to come?"

"It would've been nice, but Aunt Kay is more important."

"Come on, Shelby, I don't believe Kay is that fragile!"

"Of course you don't! You're a man!"

"Hey, I can understand feelings, but it looked to me like Kay was throwing a little tantrum. That's all!"

Shelby stared at him, seething. "I'm glad we're leaving if you're that insensitive!" With that, she bent down and grabbed her towel and beach bag and tromped up to the hotel.

Pete stood there staring after her. "What just happened?" he muttered. Then he decided to go find Dan and see if he knew what had happened to a sunny day on the beach.

Shelby hurried up to their room. When she reached it, she quietly inserted her card key and pushed the door open, expecting to find Kay asleep on her bed.

Instead Kay was watching CNN news on the television.

"Aunt Kay, I thought you'd be asleep."

"No, I'm not tired. Why did you come up so soon? I thought you and Pete were going back into the water."

"I thought you were upset and I decided I should find out what was wrong. Are you okay?"

"Yes. I was just worried about getting too sunburned."

Since her aunt looked away from her when she answered, Shelby was sure she wasn't telling the truth. She sat down on her bed, across from Kay's. That's when she noticed the tray on the bedside table between them.

"What's this?" she asked, waving her hand toward the tray.

"Oh. Dan sent me the most delicious drink. It's a little different from the one we had last night, but I really like it. Do you want to order one?"

"No, that's all right. So Dan didn't upset you?"

Again, Kay looked away. "He may have irritated me a little, but not enough for you to give up your fun."

"How did he irritate you?" Shelby leaned toward her aunt, determined to find out what Dan had done.

"He wanted to talk to me about opening a shop here in Hawaii. I told him I had a perfectly good store in Cleveland, so why would I do such a thing." She kept her gaze on the television, as if the news were riveting.

"He didn't give you any personal reasons?"

That caused her aunt's eyes to swing back to Shelby's face. "What do you mean?"

"He didn't want you to stay because he…he has feelings for you?"

Kay laughed. "I should have known. Sweetheart, you are such a romantic! But Dan and I are just friends. Of course not."

"Oh." Now Shelby was really confused. Dan hadn't been acting as if they were just friends. Why had his words about her store upset Kay? "Do you really not intend to go on the dinner cruise tonight?"

"Oh, I'll probably go. After all, he's already gotten the tickets. It would be a shame to waste them."

"I was afraid I'd find you packing, ready to go home," Shelby said slowly. "You're still okay with finishing out our vacation here?"

"Of course I am! What a waste of money that would be! I can't imagine anything so awful that I wouldn't want to finish a Hawaiian vacation. Besides, you need some time to deal with Cordy's death." She gave Shelby a smile. "And to get a tan after being cooped up studying the past three years."

"Well, I'm all for staying, as long as Dan isn't

ruining your trip. But I'd give up anything for you to be happy, Aunt Kay. I owe you so much!"

"No, dear, you owe me nothing. Having you with me has been a joy, I can assure you."

"You're the only person I know who could think taking on the job of raising a teenager not your own would be a joy."

"Well, you were such a special teenager, Shelby. Not only were you bright, but you were always grateful. You never did anything I asked you not to do. My friends all thought you were perfect, and I think they were right."

Shelby crossed to Kay's bed and leaned over to give her a hug. "Somehow, you made everything seem easier. But I feel bad that you don't have any children of your own. If you got married now, you could still have children," she suggested.

Kay grinned. "Can you imagine me pregnant? I'm so short, I'd look dreadful!"

"I think you'd look beautiful! And your child would be the luckiest kid in the world."

"Thank you, Shelby. But I don't think we have to worry about that happening."

"I don't know. Dan is too old for you, of course, but he certainly seems to like you. Maybe you haven't tried hard enough. I bet there are a lot of men in Cleveland who would like to date you."

"I don't think—" But Kay's reply was stopped by a knock on the door. "Who could that be?"

Chapter Four

Pete knocked on the door before he inserted his key and opened it.

Dan was sitting in a chair next to the desk, on the phone. From what he was saying, it was definitely a business call, but he looked up at Pete in surprise.

As soon as he hung up the phone, he asked, "What are you doing up here? I thought you and Shelby were going back in the water?"

"I thought so, too. Before I knew it, we had a fight and she went up to join her aunt."

"What did you fight about?"

"I'm not sure. But she came to the conclusion that you had flirted with her aunt but really weren't interested in her in that way and had hurt her feelings. She felt sure her aunt would be upstairs packing."

Dan raised his eyebrows. "Do you think she was right?"

"No. That was part of the problem. I said I thought her aunt was just throwing a tantrum."

Dan grinned. "That was a mistake."

"You don't have to tell me! Before I knew it, she was going upstairs to help her aunt pack."

"She wants to leave?" Dan asked, frowning.

"I didn't think so, but she'll do whatever her aunt wants her to do."

"Yeah. I like that about her."

"Why? It seems a little bizarre to me."

"It won't when you hear the story behind it."

"So tell me."

"Shelby's mother was half-crazy. But she seemed to do a fair job of raising her as long as her dad wasn't around. When he came around, Cordelia, her mother, turned into a full-fledged crazy woman. But otherwise, she wasn't bad. Until she married again. When Shelby was fourteen and home with her stepfather, he tried to rape her. Shelby was fighting and screaming at the top of her lungs when her mother and Kay came in."

"That's terrible!" Pete said.

"It got worse. Her mother blamed her for trying to seduce her husband. I don't know what would've happened if Kay hadn't been there. She told Shelby to go pack her things, and she's lived with Kay since that day."

"You're right. I do understand now why she's protective of Kay. But I still don't want her to leave yet," Pete said.

"Why?"

"You know why. She's very attractive and a lot of fun. I'm enjoying showing her the island. I think that was part of that mysterious plan you said you didn't have."

Dan grinned again. "You mean I didn't convince you?"

"No. Nor did you convince Shelby. She also has a very sharp brain."

"Yeah, I know."

"You seem to know an awful lot about Shelby," Pete said, staring at Dan.

"It comes from corresponding with Kay. She's very proud of her only chick." Dan stared across the room, thinking about how much he owed Kay.

"Dan?"

He looked back at Pete. "Yeah?"

"Should we call and see if they're leaving?"

"I've got a better idea. Why don't you send Shelby a tray like I sent Kay?"

After hearing Dan's suggestion, Pete thought of an addition that might give them the energy for the dinner cruise. He added fresh pineapple and two slices of coconut cake, the hotel chef's specialty. He asked the waiter to bring it by his room so he could add a personal note to it. Then he followed the waiter to Shelby's floor.

He waited by the elevator while the tray was delivered. When the waiter returned, Pete asked his question.

"Were they packing?"

"No, sir, I didn't see any signs of suitcases. They

were sitting on their beds talking and the television was on." They both got in the elevator, and Pete pushed the button for his floor.

"Oh, and I forgot to tell you they liked the desserts," the waiter said.

Pete reached in his pocket and gave him an additional tip. "Thanks."

"But, sir, you've already given me a tip, and the ladies gave me another one."

"Then it's your lucky day, isn't it? Keep the tips. You've earned them."

"We need to decide what to wear if we're definitely going," Shelby said after she'd finished the delicious cake Pete had sent them.

Kay stretched out across her bed. "I suppose you're right. What do you have to wear this evening?"

"My black dress is my only choice. What are you going to wear?"

"I guess the pale blue, though it will go unnoticed beside you," Kay said with a smile.

"Maybe not to everyone," Shelby said, watching her aunt.

"Don't start talking about that silly idea again. I told you Dan and I are just friends."

"But—"

Kay put up a hand to quiet her. "But nothing. Now, you'd better get in the shower and get ready. I don't want to hear another word about any of this."

Shelby did as she was told, but she still wasn't convinced. She intended to stick to Kay's side this evening to see if she was lying to her. No one was going to make her aunt unhappy without paying for it!

Pete had fallen asleep on his bed. When he awoke, Dan had come out of the bathroom, dressed in a navy-blue suit. "Am I running late?"

"No, I was about to awaken you so you'd have time in the shower. We still have about half an hour, but I have to go down and buy the tickets."

Pete frowned. "Didn't you tell Kay you'd already bought them?"

"I lied. I thought she'd be less likely to cancel if she thought I'd lose money."

"That was quick thinking, but what if they find out?"

"I'll explain that I wanted to see her," Dan said with a shrug of his shoulders.

Pete immediately picked up on something. "Her? Do you mean Kay?"

"Of course I mean Kay."

"Shelby says she's too young for you," Pete warned.

"Shelby *is* too young for me."

"Not Shelby, Kay."

"She is. I'm just showing her Hawaii. Then she'll go back to Cleveland and that will be that."

There was something in Dan's voice that bothered Pete. Disappointment maybe? "Did you think she'd open a shop here and stay?"

"It was a possibility, but she rejected that idea."

"Maybe you need to give her more time," Pete said,

knowing that if Kay stayed, Shelby would consider staying, too. He liked that idea.

"Maybe you'd better get in the shower or you'll miss the boat." After he said that, Dan opened the door and disappeared.

Pete grabbed his things and got in the shower. He wasn't going to be left behind.

When the two men knocked on the women's door at five-thirty, the time agreed upon for ascending to the lounge on the top floor for the requisite view of Diamond Head, they waited impatiently for the door to open.

When it did, Pete was treated to a vision named Shelby.

He stared at her, completely stunned. She was wearing a black dress that left her shoulders bare, held up only by a shoestring strap on each side.

But the most astonishing part was her hair. She'd worn it in a braid continuously. Tonight it was a glorious wave of red curls almost to her waist. There were two small stars in her hair to hold it back from her face.

All he could do was stare.

"Pete? Is something wrong?" Shelby asked when he didn't move.

"Your hair…"

"I know. It can be a mess, but I thought for tonight it would be all right." Shelby sounded almost apologetic for her stunning beauty.

Dan took a satisfied Kay by the arm, only saying, "Of course, it will be fine."

Pete turned to stare at his mentor. Was the man insane? Her hair would be fine? It was more than fine. He wanted to wrap it around himself. He wanted to run his fingers through it and never let go. He wanted to take her arm and lead her straight to his room.

Instead he followed Dan and Kay to the elevator. He took Shelby's hand and held it in his, as if afraid she'd get away. He felt as if he were escorting a fairy that might fly away at any moment.

Such a fanciful thought surprised him. He'd never been poetic in his life. But he wished he could collapse on one knee and use poetry to pay homage to her.

"Is everything all right?" Shelby asked him.

"Uh, yeah, everything's fine."

Just before the doors of the elevator opened, he whispered to her, "You look beautiful tonight."

She just smiled at him and stepped out of the elevator.

Her hair was like a magnet, attracting all eyes. He kept a tight hold on her hand, determined to fight off the hordes of men he expected to descend upon them.

As soon as they sat down, a waiter appeared and asked their drink preferences. All but Shelby ordered a glass of wine. She asked for mineral water.

"You don't care for wine?"

She looked up at Pete's question. "My mother was an alcoholic. I avoid alcohol as a general rule."

Pete was left with nothing to say.

It was Dan who answered. "Wise decision," he said softly before he turned his attention to Kay. "You look very nice in that color. It matches your eyes."

"That's kind of you, Dan. I didn't expect compliments after anyone saw Shelby. Isn't she beautiful?"

"Kay, you're embarrassing me!" Shelby protested.

Dan smiled at her. "Kay is a great mother, isn't she?"

"The best," Shelby agreed. "In fact, we were talking about that today. I think Kay should start looking for a husband when we get back home. She's still young enough to have several children of her own. And they would be so lucky to have her as a mother."

"Shelby!" Kay protested.

After studying Kay for a moment, Dan said, "I believe you're right, Shelby. And I shouldn't think it would be hard to find a man to marry Kay. They'll probably be lined up at her door."

"My thoughts exactly," Shelby concurred.

Kay quieted them. "You're both being silly and embarrassing me. Tell me, Pete," she said, looking at the crater in the distance, "do a lot of people climb Diamond Head? It looks difficult."

Pete, who had been staring at Shelby, pulled himself together to answer. "Uh, yeah. One of the guidebooks said it was an easy climb, but it's not, especially on a hot day. But you'll find a lot of tourists doing it, even with babies or toddlers."

"But there is a path, isn't there?"

"Yes, but sometimes you have to climb up steep steps, or half crawl through low-ceilinged bunkers. I can assure you this view is just as nice and much easier to reach." He ended with a smile.

"And I would guess we'd be exhausted and hot and

sweaty if we did the climb the hard way. And then we wouldn't look as nice, would we?" Kay asked.

Pete and Dan laughed. Then Dan said, "Definitely not, Kay, and we much appreciate the way you look tonight." Then he raised her hand to his lips and kissed it.

Pete noticed Kay's cheeks flushing. He turned to discover Shelby staring at the couple. "Shelby, do—"

"Excuse me. I wondered if the lady would like to dance?"

All four of them stared at the dark-haired man in a tux who was staring at Shelby.

Shelby smiled and was about to say, No, thank you.

At the same time, Pete growled, "No, she doesn't!"

The man gave a small nod and walked away.

Shelby, however, wasn't willing to let the incident end there. "How dare you answer for me? He directed the question at me, so I had the right to answer him."

Pete knew at once he'd made a mistake. "Yes, of course, you're right. I was just trying to protect you."

Shelby was still enraged. "I don't need your protection!"

Dan intervened. "Shelby, I think you're overreacting. Tonight you're Pete's guest. He was just taking care of you."

"Since you are not my parent, Dan, I think you have no right to try to control my behavior."

"But I do, my dear," Kay said softly. "And Dan is right. You shouldn't blame Pete for thinking he needed to protect you. After all, you look like an innocent, you know."

Shelby could never resist Kay's request, spoken or unspoken, so she sat back against the couch. "All right, I'll forgive you, Pete, but you should know that I can take care of myself and will answer all questions that are addressed to me."

"Maybe I should explain that Shelby is an expert in self-defense," Kay said, smiling at Pete. "It's been a regimen that has produced excellent conditioning as well as self-confidence."

Pete turned to Shelby. "You mean you could take down a man who was being too, uh, amorous?"

"Yes," was Shelby's succinct answer.

Staring at her, he muttered, "Good thing to know."

After a few more minutes Dan said they should go, since it was almost time to board the boat. "We want to pick out the best table, of course."

"Don't we have a table reserved?" Kay asked.

"Well, sort of, but we can choose one of several tables in an area. I like to choose what I think will be the best."

And they did. The table was on deck, as were numerous others, but it was almost by itself. They settled into their chairs, and a waiter appeared beside them with a selection of drinks to enjoy as the boat slipped away from the pier.

They watched the sun set in glorious color, its beams glancing off the gentle waves of the ocean. When it had finally disappeared, hundreds of lanterns around the boat were lit, as well as candles on each table.

"Oh, this is lovely. I'm so glad we didn't miss it," Shelby said softly.

Pete leaned closer. "Me, too."

He was still bowled over by her appearance tonight, but he didn't want her to think that he was only interested in her looks. There was a great deal more to Shelby than met the eye.

After they gave their order, Pete asked Shelby to dance, since music was playing in the background.

"Where?" she asked, looking around.

"There's plenty of room on the deck. You'll see. Others will start dancing, too."

Almost as if he'd willed it, several couples from nearby tables stood to dance.

"All right. I'd love to."

Pete was a reasonably good dancer and acquitted himself well, but he'd admit to himself that his main reason for asking Shelby to dance was to get his hands on her.

When Pete's hands slid around her, one holding her hand, Shelby relaxed. He wasn't trying to force intimacy, like some men when they danced. Shelby hated that. Instead he led her gracefully through the music in an extremely romantic atmosphere.

Though she was tall, Pete was taller, and she couldn't resist resting her head on his shoulder. He pulled her a little tighter against him and slowed their steps, but she didn't mind. He felt right to her, for the first time in her life.

Lost in the music and the man, she forgot her intention to keep an eye on Kay and Dan. It was only when they came back to the table after dancing to several songs that she discovered the other two were missing.

As Pete held her chair for her and she sat down, she asked, "Where are Kay and Dan?"

"Probably dancing somewhere on the deck." He moved to his own chair and sipped his drink without concern.

With a frown Shelby looked around them, finding it difficult to see in the shadows. "Do you see them?"

"No. What's wrong?"

"I'm worried about Kay."

"She's with Dan. He'll take care of her."

After several minutes of silence, Shelby stood. "I need to go find Kay."

Pete stood also. "That's crazy, Shelby. You could search for hours and never find them if they don't want you to. And if they aren't hiding, they'll show up any minute, and you'll be the one missing then."

"You don't understand. I was going to keep a close eye on those two, to make sure he didn't upset Kay."

"I'm sure he won't."

"Why are you sure? He certainly did a good job upsetting her this afternoon! Don't you remember?"

"You're the one who decided she was upset. She wasn't packing when you got upstairs."

"Maybe not, but something was wrong. I can't figure out what's going on between the two of them. But I will."

Chapter Five

"What do you think of Shelby's idea?" Dan asked as he stood beside Kay on the boat deck, watching as darkness fell on the waves.

Kay, who seemed lost in the beauty of the moment, looked up in surprise. "What idea was that?"

"The one where you find a husband and have several kids right away."

Kay shrugged her shoulders. "That was just Shelby's fantasy. She's a great romantic, in spite of her past."

"Why not marry and have children? Don't you want to have a baby?"

"If it happens, it would be nice, but I'm not going to act like a crazy person, looking for a husband wherever I can find one. I won't be tied down to someone I don't respect."

"Don't you think someone could come along that you do respect? Someone who might want a family, too?"

"I don't think it's a man's first priority."

"What is his first priority?" Dan asked.

Kay shrugged her shoulders. "Sex."

"Some men look for more than just sex, Kay. Surely you know that."

"I know that this is a ridiculous discussion to be having here in Hawaii on a beautiful night. I think the air is perfumed, don't you?"

"It is. It's all the flowers on the island. I gather you don't want to discuss serious things?"

"No, I don't. That shouldn't come as a surprise since I'm on vacation."

"All right." He took her arm and turned her toward him. "Then we'll dance."

She came into his arms, fitting perfectly, as if destined to be his dancing partner. "Isn't it strange that I've never danced with you, though I've known you a long time?"

He gathered her into his arms and began moving with the music. "Not really. You were pretty young when I knew you. Much too young to be dancing with me."

"Besides which, Cordy would've killed me," Kay replied with a sad laugh.

"Yeah. I didn't realize how depressed she was. I guess I was too young to recognize it."

"Yes. No one could've saved her."

Dan recalled from Kay's letters that Cordelia had been single when she'd died, her second husband having left her years before. The circumstances of her death were still fresh in his mind. "I'm sorry she was alone when—"

Kay gazed up at him, an odd look in her eye. "She wasn't, unfortunately. They found her with two men. All of them had overdosed. I'm sorry. I never told Shelby, either. I didn't think knowing the gruesome details would help anything."

"You're very protective of a young woman who says she can take out anyone," Dan pointed out. A small smile was on his lips.

"She is strong, but she shouldn't have to deal with things like that."

"And you should?"

She laid her head against his shoulder. "There wasn't anyone else," she said softly.

He dropped her hand and cuddled her against him, more like am embrace than a dance. But he didn't care. "I should've been there."

"No," she said with a sigh. "It wouldn't have helped. Cordy was on a downward spiral. I'm just glad she didn't take Shelby down with her."

"Thanks to you," Dan whispered, and kissed her forehead.

"Aunt Kay!" Shelby's shrill voice startled the couple. "What are you doing?"

Though Kay stiffened and pulled away, Dan didn't let her go. He looked over at Shelby calmly; she hadn't caught him doing anything wrong. "We were reminiscing. Is that a problem?"

Shelby stared at him, suddenly realizing his eyes were the same color blue as her own. "No, not if that's what Kay wants to do."

"She wasn't protesting, Shelby. I would never force her to do anything she doesn't want to do." Kay, he noticed, stayed behind him, though. She let him do the talking.

"Well, they're…they're serving our meal now," Shelby stuttered. "I thought you'd want to know."

Dan nodded. "Yes, thank you. We'll be there in a minute."

After Pete, who had followed Shelby, led her back to their table, Dan turned to Kay. "She really is protective of you, isn't she?"

"Yes. But if you'll remember, I'm her only parent now. It will take her a while to accept that."

With his arm still around her, Dan moved them along the deck back to their table.

Shelby, he noted, was watching for them.

"I thought you said our meal was here," Dan said as he sat down.

"I thought it was coming. They brought the bread." Shelby gave him a challenging look.

Dan gave her a warm smile. "Then, by all means, pass us the bread."

Pete watched Shelby throughout the meal. He'd become used to Shelby's mood changes. From the romantic young woman he'd held in his arms, she'd become a determined protector of her aunt.

What had him confused was Dan's behavior.

He appeared completely involved with Kay. Was that part of his plan? While Dan hadn't actually explained his plan, Pete definitely believed there was one.

He felt sure Dan had wanted him to get to know Shelby. To enjoy and share her companionship. What he didn't know was how far his friend wanted him to go. He was sure he wasn't supposed to bed Shelby, though that idea intrigued him. Just holding her in his arms while they danced gave him ideas that he didn't think were proper.

Now he could tell that Shelby had completely forgotten any of the feelings he'd hoped she'd experienced on the dance floor. She was totally focused on Kay and Dan. His attempts at chitchat were ignored.

"Shelby!"

When she finally turned to look at him, Pete couldn't think of a thing to say. "Uh, do you like your dinner?"

"It's fine, thank you, Pete."

"I think it'll be a minute before they bring the dessert. Want to take another spin around the floor?"

"I suppose we could, as long as we don't go far. We should stay within sight of the table so we don't miss our dessert."

"Sure, yeah. We'll stay close." He glanced at Dan and saw approval in his eyes.

Shelby, throwing a few strands of red curls back over her shoulder, moved into his arms, and he felt he was holding a treasure. He pulled her closer to him and swayed to the music.

"Pete?" Shelby whispered.

"Yeah, honey?" he said, focusing on other things.

"Didn't you think Dan was hugging Kay? I mean, they weren't dancing because they weren't moving."

"So?"

"Well, don't you think that's a little strange? She hasn't seen him in maybe twenty years. You wouldn't think they'd have reached the hugging stage that fast, would you?"

"I don't know. I think we did," he murmured as he held her a little closer.

She immediately pulled away from him. "No, we're dancing."

"Well, yeah, but it's almost the same."

"They're bringing the desserts. We should return to the table."

Before he could protest, she'd pulled from his arms and headed to her seat.

All of them concentrated on their coconut cake, with no conversation. When they had all finished, Shelby said, "Well, it's been a lovely evening. Thank you so much, Dan, Pete. I'm sure we'll see you before we leave." She stood up. "Ready, Kay?"

"Darling, I'm ready when you are, but unless you can walk on water, I suggest we wait until the boat docks." Kay held back a smile.

"Oh!" Shelby responded, her cheeks flushing as she realized her error.

"That's the problem with dinner cruises," Dan said. "You can't leave until the cruise ends."

Shelby recovered quickly. Her tone was icy when she asked, "And just when will that be?"

Dan looked at his watch. "I believe we're scheduled to dock at ten. Until then, they have music and dancing and a singer to entertain you."

"Then shall we all move inside so we can listen to the singer?" Shelby suggested, obviously hoping Kay agreed with her.

"I guess we could do that," Kay agreed, looking at Dan for his opinion.

"Of course we will, Kay, if that's what you want to do."

All four of them moved into the main lounge where a small stage and dance floor were surrounded by tables and chairs. They selected a table near the dance floor and Pete immediately asked Shelby to dance again.

"I don't think—"

"Oh, go on, Shelby," Kay urged. "We'll be right here, I promise."

Shelby reluctantly agreed, and Pete led her to the floor. He let out a sigh of relief when he felt her against him again. He was beginning to think he was addicted to Shelby Cook.

The scent of her wreathed around him, enveloped him. "How long is your vacation?" he whispered.

"Two weeks, at least that's what it was when we left home."

"Have you done much studying since you got here?"

"An hour here and there. But Kay wants me to participate in whatever she does…and she's been busy with Dan."

For which Pete was grateful. "Which means I've

had time with you. Though I'm not sure how much time off work we'll have next week." They were set to negotiate a major deal with a new client that would increase their business ten percent. As much as he had been instrumental in bringing about the deal, he hadn't given it much thought in the last few days.

Shelby sounded truly apologetic when she said, "We shouldn't have been taking up so much of your time. I'll tell Kay that, too."

"No, don't do that. It would upset Dan. He'll decide how much time he can spend entertaining Kay next week, not me."

"But it's possible he'll have to work longer hours next week?"

"It's possible. I was surprised when we took off early today. But I enjoyed it…until you cut it short. I was hoping to teach you to surf."

"You can surf?"

"Of course. I'm a native. I was practically raised on a board. I could teach you, if you want."

"Oh, I'd love that. Maybe we could do it in the morning one day."

"Really? How about tomorrow? I don't have anything important scheduled." He hoped Dan would forgive him for that small lie.

"Are you sure? I don't want to get you in trouble," Shelby said.

"No, it's not a problem. Shall I pick you up at eight?"

"I'd love it, if you think I can learn."

"Oh, yeah, I believe you can learn."

* * *

On the way home that evening, after they'd escorted the ladies back to their hotel room, Pete said, "Dan, I think we need to talk."

"About what?" Dan asked as he drove to Pete's apartment.

"I think it's time you came clean with me, and that you also came clean about that almighty plan."

"Why?"

"Because I don't like working blind. You brought me into this situation without telling me the facts. I think I at least deserve that."

Dan sighed. "I suppose you're right, but you'd better be sure you're ready for the truth. Because you can't go back once you've heard it all."

"I'm ready."

They both entered Pete's apartment, overlooking the Pacific.

Dan said, after looking around, "You're a lot tidier than usual."

"The cleaning lady came today."

"Oh, I see."

"Sit down. Do you want something to drink?"

"No, thanks. Let's get this over with."

"You make it sound like you're facing a firing squad."

"Nothing that bad. But you'll think a lot worse of me when you hear the truth."

Pete frowned. He'd always admired Dan, ever since he was a teen, and he couldn't think of anything that would change that fact. "I don't believe that."

Dan gave him a bittersweet look. "I know you don't."

"So tell me what you've done that is so horrible."

"I abandoned my child."

"You have a child? Where is it?"

"You don't know?" Dan stared at him, waiting.

"How would I—" He broke off as realization flooded him. "Shelby? You can't mean Shelby!"

"I'm afraid so."

"But you told her you didn't know her father."

"I lied."

"How could you do that?"

Dan let out a big sigh and stood to pace across the room. "You had to be there."

"Tell me." He needed to know. Right now it seemed to him as if the statue had fallen off its pedestal and he needed to set things right again.

Without hesitation Dan explained, "I had unprotected sex with her mother. That is, her mother told me she was protected. She wasn't. When she told me she was carrying my child, I married her."

Pete nodded, agreeing with Dan's choice.

"Our marriage was hell. I tried. Damn, I tried until I thought I'd go crazy. Shelby was born and things were okay for a couple of months. Then her mother started up again. Only now, she was going out most nights, leaving me home with Kay, who was only ten and our baby.

"When Shelby was two years old, I told Cordelia I wanted a divorce. I was confident she wouldn't want the baby, since she was out most nights. Even if she should want the baby, I didn't think the judge would let her have her."

He came back and sat down. "I was wrong on both counts. Cordelia insisted she wanted custody and as the mother she'd be the best person to raise Shelby. I didn't have a good attorney. I didn't think I'd need one. It all seemed so simple to me. But it wasn't. The judge gave Cordelia custody."

Pete shook his head in disbelief. "The court always prefers the mother."

"Well, the judge was wrong." Hurt and anger still sounded in his tone. "Kay thought I'd be better with Shelby. But that didn't matter."

"So is that when you came to Hawaii?"

"No, I waited a couple of years. Cordelia's parents had died in a car crash and Kay was living with us at the time of our divorce. Almost all care of Shelby fell to Kay after the divorce. Which made it easier for me to see Shelby, until one night Cordelia came home early to find me visiting with my daughter."

"That must have been difficult."

Dan gave a bitter laugh. "That's an understatement."

"Is that when you left?"

"Not quite. Kay promised she'd call me. She didn't get to do so until days later. She told me she couldn't risk letting me see Shelby. That's when I left. I had to get away. I couldn't stay in Cleveland anymore, knowing I couldn't see my own child out of fear for what Cordelia would do to her. For her sake, I got as far away as possible."

Pete saw the toll that remembering the past was taking on Dan. Suddenly he looked ten years older.

But he continued. "Kay promised to take care of Shelby, and said she would write me if I'd let her know where I was. She gave me her friend's address and asked me to mail letters to her there. Which I did until she moved out of Cordelia's home."

"When was that?"

"When she went to college. Even during the summers, she took classes and remained in the dorm. But she had Shelby over to college with her a lot."

"I guess you were really relieved when she took Shelby into her house to live."

"Yes, I was. I'd been giving her some money to spend on Shelby, but when she took her in, I paid for everything."

"Is that how Shelby paid for law school?"

"I paid for most of it, but I'm sure Kay helped her, too. But Shelby doesn't know that."

"No, I'd guess not since she doesn't even know you're her father. Didn't she even have any pictures of you?"

"Cordelia destroyed all of them. My visits were so early in her life and so traumatic, I'm sure she doesn't remember anything about me." Dan ran a hand though his hair and hung his head. "So now you know everything, my friend." That said, he headed for the front door.

"Not so fast," Pete called out to him.

"What is it?"

"I want to know the same thing your daughter wants to know."

"And what is that?"

"Your intentions toward Kay."

"You think I would do anything to hurt Kay?"

Pete almost took a step back when he saw the fierce look on Dan's face. "No, but I'm working without a net here. What if I make Shelby *more* suspicious of you?"

"I don't see how you could make her *more* suspicious of me!"

"Maybe not, but I think I could help make her less suspicious of you, now that I know the truth."

"I doubt that."

"So hugging Kay was just a way to pass the time?" Pete goaded him.

"No!"

"Then explain yourself."

Dan let out a big sigh before he sat back down. "Okay, okay. The truth is…I don't know."

"What do you mean you don't know? You have to know."

"Look, I've always been fond of Kay, and through the years, we kind of used our letter writing like a diary. I probably know her better now than anyone on earth."

"And…?"

"And I know she's a wonderful person."

"That doesn't tell me anything."

"I know."

"I think you're in love with her."

Dan shook his head. "I'm way too old for her. You heard what Shelby's been telling her. She should return home and find someone to marry her, give her kids."

"So? What's to stop you from being that guy?"

"About twelve years."

"Is that how much older you are than her?"

"Yeah. I stand next to her and I feel the weight of my years."

"She doesn't seem to notice. Shouldn't you give her the chance to decide if she thinks you're too old for her?"

"It would be embarrassing for both of us if I made her say it. It's obvious she isn't interested."

"How do you know?"

"She doesn't give me any lingering glances. She doesn't flirt with me."

That wasn't the way Pete saw it. "She sure wasn't protesting when you were hugging her this evening."

"That's because we were talking about Cordy's death and her having to deal with it. I was apologizing for her having to handle all of it alone."

"It wasn't your job anymore," Pete said, trying to comfort his friend. "How about her second husband?"

"No. Kay said they'd divorced several years ago."

"I didn't think to ask how she died. I mean, she was so young."

"She was a year younger than me. She died of a drug overdose…with two men who died from the same cause."

"Did Shelby—"

"No. Kay took care of everything and didn't tell Shelby about the circumstances of her mother's death."

Pete's mind struggled to process all the information. When it all started to sink in, he asked, "And Kay decided to bring Shelby here so you could get to know her?"

"Yes. We'd talked about it years ago, but she thought it would cause Shelby too much trouble with her mother if we didn't wait. Cordy was still in touch with Shelby until her death."

"And you didn't ever try to see Shelby after she moved in with Kay?"

"No. Kay asked me not to. She said Shelby still had a relationship with her mother, and Kay thought that was important. It would've ended if Cordy learned that I had come to see Shelby."

"So, now what?"

Dan gave him a blank look.

"You haven't told her you're her father. Why not?"

"Her mother told her so many lies about me, Kay thinks she would reject me out of hand. She thinks it will be easier if Shelby gets to know me."

"That's not going to happen as long as she thinks you're leading Kay on."

"But I'm not!"

"I know that, and you know that, but Shelby doesn't know that." Pete put a comforting hand on his friend's shoulder. "You'll have to find a way to win Shelby over if you're ever going to get to know her."

Chapter Six

The beach was almost deserted, save for a few surfers already out in the ocean, waiting for waves. At eight o'clock tourists were still sleeping, especially here on Sunset Beach, a fair ride from Waikiki.

Shelby licked her lips in a nervous gesture. "Do you really think I can learn to surf?"

"Of course you can," Pete assured her as he parked the car. "Unless I'm a rotten teacher. As Kay pointed out, you're in great shape." He walked around back and handed her a life jacket from the backseat of the convertible. "But I want you to wear this anyway."

"Why?"

Pete laughed. "Because Kay would kill me if anything happened to you. If you go under, you'll pop back up with the vest on. That way I can find you at once."

"I think you worry too much about what Kay thinks, but I'll go along with you since you're giving me free surfing lessons."

"Hmm," he said as he took his surfboard out. "Did I say they were free?"

"Didn't you?"

"Well, I don't take cash. I thought maybe you could pay in kisses rather than money."

Shelby gave him a stare. Then, to his surprise, she played along. "Possibly, but it depends on how good you are."

"I'll be on my best behavior today. Come on, let's get in the water."

Pete was eager to get his hands on Shelby. She looked great this morning, even though her hair was braided again. Her trim figure was outlined in the blue one-piece she wore, and he noticed that several of the surfers paid way too much attention to his student.

Once they were about waist deep, he laid his board into the water and began telling her where she should stand.

Then he got seated on the board before he helped Shelby to sit in front of him. They paddled out a little so they could catch a wave and ride it in. After several wipeouts, they caught a ride, and Pete enjoyed it more than any other, because his arms were around Shelby.

When they took a break, floating on the board in the ocean, several of the other surfers, whom Pete knew, circled them.

"Hey, Pete, introduce us to the lady," one of them said.

"This is Shelby. It's her first trip to the islands."

"Hey, Shelby," several guys called out.

Shelby smiled and waved back. They drew closer.

"If you really want to learn to surf, I should teach you," one of the guys offered.

"No way, Johnny," Pete returned. "I'll do all the teaching Shelby needs." He managed to turn the surfboard around and head back out to catch another wave.

"Pete, don't you want some time to yourself?" Shelby asked as he paddled through the water. "I can sit on the beach and watch if you do."

"I can surf after you've gone back to Cleveland. Besides, I'm not leaving you alone on the beach. You'd be surrounded by all those surf bums in no time. They'd give up surfing to spend time with you, too."

"You're exaggerating," Shelby said with a laugh.

For the next couple of hours they surfed and laughed, and Pete had never enjoyed himself more. Shelby was a quick learner, but more important she was a perfect companion. The sassy, suspicious woman never made an appearance; instead he was treated to her sweet, sexy alter ego. The woman he adored.

"Oh, that was wonderful!" Shelby exclaimed as she slumped back against the seat in Pete's convertible. "Thank you so much."

"It was my pleasure." And he wasn't lying. Teaching her to surf was the perfect excuse to put his hands on her waist, to hold her against him. He loved the feel of her. "You were great, Shelby."

"Thanks. I think my self-defense training paid off for me again. You know, Kay put me in the classes at the suggestion of the psychologist I saw after...a bad incident early in my teen years. The classes gave me strength, balance and confidence."

"I can see that. That confidence will make you a good trial lawyer." He could just picture her in front of a jury, with her hair in curls down to her waist. No man would vote against her.

"I plan to go into corporate law."

"Oh, I see. Hey, I think Dan needs a corporate attorney. You could take that job and remain in Hawaii. I don't have to tell you I'd be in favor of that move, do I?"

"That's very sweet of you, Pete, but I don't think Dan would accept me without a strict review of my qualifications which would not involve my athletic ability."

"Let's go ask him!" Pete exclaimed and made a quick turn onto another coastal roadway.

"What are you doing? I told Kay I'd be back around noon."

"Actually, Dan asked me to bring you by for a few minutes. He wanted to talk to you without Kay being around."

"Why?"

"He's the one who has to explain, but I'll stay with you." When she looked edgy, he quickly reassured her. "You won't be in any danger."

"I didn't think I would be, but I can't think what he

would want to talk to me about, especially without Kay being there."

Suddenly she turned to stare at him. From her expression he was pretty sure she figured it out.

"You mean he wants to talk to me about Kay?"

After a quick glance at her stunned expression, Pete pressed down on the accelerator, hoping to reach Dan quickly.

"Wait a minute! I don't want to talk to Dan about Kay. My loyalty belongs to her, not Dan!"

"Just give him a chance to explain, Shelby. I promise he doesn't want to hurt Kay. That's just not in him."

Shelby sat stiffly in the car, staring straight ahead. There was no further conversation, no easy companionship of the sort he'd enjoyed during their morning together.

When he stopped in front of Dan's house, Shelby finally spoke. "What is this? Aren't we going to the office?"

"No. Dan asked me to bring you to his home."

Pete had known she'd be impressed. Who wouldn't be? Dan had a beautiful place on the beach. You couldn't tell a lot from the front because it was surrounded by palm trees and dense foliage, but when she walked in, the house would stun her.

"Come on, Shelby. Dan's got a great place."

She got out of the car, but reluctance was in her every move.

He'd accomplished his assignment, so he didn't try to change her mind. That was Dan's job, not his.

* * *

Shelby dreaded stepping into Dan's house. She felt as if she were entering the enemy's lair. Dan expected something from her to do with Kay. He was crazy. She'd never help him bring Kay into his clutches.

After Pete rang the doorbell, they waited in silence. A woman, obviously a native Hawaiian, opened the door. She smiled broadly when she saw Pete.

"Hi, Betty. Is Dan in?"

"Of course, and he's waiting for you. Come with me."

They entered the house, and she led them to the living room, which covered most of the length of the house. Lined with floor-to-ceiling windows, the room looked out on the beach. Shelby stood for a moment to take it all in.

"This is a beautiful room," she said softly.

"Thank you, Shelby," a deep voice replied.

Her head snapped up and she saw Dan entering from a different door. "I didn't see you, Dan."

"I know. Thank you, Betty."

The woman nodded and left the room.

"Betty is my housekeeper. She does an excellent job," Dan explained. He motioned to an overstuffed white sofa that faced the Pacific. "Won't you sit down?"

"I don't think I should," Shelby said, the stiffness she'd felt earlier returning to her voice. "I don't intend to tell you anything about Kay that you don't already know. And I don't plot against her."

"Even if it's for her own good?"

"What do you mean?"

"If you'll sit, I'll explain," Dan said easily.

She sat down, Pete joining her, but even Dan could see she wasn't convinced.

Dan sat in a chair and leaned forward. "I've been doing a lot of thinking about what you said."

"What did I say?"

"That Kay is still young enough to marry and have her own family. I hadn't thought of that. She's been such a strong person, I forget she's still young."

"Yes, she is." She was still suspicious, but Shelby had to admit he'd won her over a little.

"But I think Kay is shy with strangers. I don't think she'll even consider going out of her way to find a husband, so I'm worried about it ever happening for her."

Dan lost ground with Shelby when he criticized Kay. She stiffened and raised her chin in a defiant gesture.

"I'm going to help her, once we get back to Cleveland."

"So you know a lot of men Kay's age?" Dan asked.

"No, but I'll find some."

Dan gave a her a smile, one she'd classify as smug. "I already know a number of men Kay's age or a little older, and I thought maybe I could host a party for Kay to meet them. She wouldn't be the least bit suspicious."

Shelby paused before she answered. "That's very thoughtful of you, Dan, and I appreciate your desire to help, but you must have forgotten that all these men will remain in Hawaii and Kay will not."

Now it was Dan's turn to pause. "I understand that Kay's remaining in Hawaii isn't what you expected,

Shelby. But would you deny her the opportunity to find happiness because it doesn't fit your plans?"

Shelby's cheeks flushed. "No, I wouldn't do that! But— All right, I see your point." It killed her to admit it, but Dan was right. Hadn't she herself often worried that she'd gotten in the way of Kay having a life, a family of her own? She didn't think Kay would choose to stay in the islands, but at least she could get her feet wet, so to speak, with a few dates.

"Good. Tomorrow is Wednesday, and Betty says she can have things ready by then. So at lunch today I'll invite both of you to my little get-together."

"At lunch today?" Shelby asked, a question in her eyes.

"I called Kay earlier and told her I would send a car for her to join us here for lunch. I hope that was all right. Kay agreed."

"I wish I'd known. I'd have brought something to change into."

"Kay said she'd bring something for you. She should be here any minute."

"You didn't think it would take long to convince me, did you?" Shelby demanded.

"You're a logical woman with a warm heart. I knew you'd do something good for Kay. I trusted in your generosity."

Just then the doorbell rang.

"That will be Kay. I'll get it, Betty," Dan called as he moved eagerly to the door.

For the first time since they arrived, Pete leaned

forward and spoke. "You did great, Shelby. Dan really wants to help Kay."

"I know."

"Oh, Dan, this is gorgeous!" Kay exclaimed as she entered the house.

"Thanks. I'm glad you like it."

Shelby stood and greeted her aunt. "Did you bring clothes for me?"

"I did. Sorry I couldn't bring a change for you, Pete."

"I've got some clothes in the car. I'll go get them." Pete strode to the front door and out.

"If you'll point out the closest bathroom, Dan, I'll go change, too," Shelby said.

Dan called Betty, and the housekeeper appeared at once. "Shelby needs to change, if you'll show her to a bedroom."

"Of course. Right this way, miss."

Shelby followed the housekeeper out of the room.

Kay's gaze followed Shelby's departure. "Is something wrong with Shelby?"

"No. Why do you ask?"

"She just seemed…subdued, somehow."

"The waves can take a lot out of you." When he heard Betty come back down the hall, he asked, "Betty, can you bring some fruit drinks for all four of us? I think the surfers need some restoring."

"Of course, Mr. Dan."

Kay wandered around the room. "Your housekeeper seems very nice, and she's obviously very efficient. Your house is as clean as clean can be."

Dan smiled. "You're so right, honey. Betty has trained me. I'm nowhere near as messy as I used to be."

Kay laughed. "Good for her. I wouldn't have thought that was possible."

"I'm a slow learner, but I get there eventually."

Both Shelby and Pete got back to the living room as Betty brought out a tray of fruit drinks.

"Oh, lovely," Shelby said as she saw the drinks.

"I bet you're hungry, too," Betty said with an appreciative smile. "Lunch won't be long in coming."

"I think we'll sit on the patio," Dan said, leading the way and holding the door open for Betty.

Once they were all sitting outside, cooled by the ocean breeze in the shade, drinking their refreshing fruit drinks, Dan mentioned that he was entertaining some friends the next night and he hoped Kay and Shelby would join them.

"Dan, you're not required to spend every night of our vacation with us," Kay said.

"It's not a case of have to, Kay. I *want* to spend the time with you. Besides, I want to show you off to all my friends. Please say you'll come."

"Is it all right with you, Shelby?" Kay asked.

"Of course. It'll be fun."

Kay turned to her host. "Is there anything we can do to help Betty prepare?"

"When she brings out lunch, we'll ask her. I haven't given her much notice this time, I'll admit."

As if on cue, Betty appeared with a large tray laden with dishes. Dan jumped up to open the door for her.

As Betty served lunch, Dan relayed Kay's kind offer.

Betty, after looking at Dan and receiving a slight nod, welcomed the help.

"We'll come to the kitchen after lunch and talk about how we can help you, Betty," Kay said. "Thank you for letting us contribute to the evening."

Lunch was delightful. The food was exceptional and conversation lively. Kay kept an eye on Shelby, but she thought Shelby's spirits had kicked back up.

After lunch Kay and Shelby carried the dishes to the kitchen.

"Oh, ma'am, you shouldn't have bothered with those," Betty protested.

"We were coming anyway, Betty. I haven't had such wonderful food since we landed. Betty, lunch was exquisite."

The housekeeper beamed at Kay. "Thank you, ma'am."

The three women put their heads together and figured out what each could do, both Kay and Shelby being careful to leave the creative parts to Betty. They promised to arrive by three the next afternoon, bringing their clothes for the party with them.

Afterward, Kay asked Pete if he could take them back to the hotel. "I promised Shelby time each day to study, so I think we'd better head back. Thank you for the wonderful lunch, Dan. Your house is absolutely fabulous."

"I'm glad you liked it. You're welcome here anytime."

Since the backseat in Pete's car was almost nonexistent, Shelby insisted her aunt sit in front with Pete. She sat sideways on the backseat with her knees drawn up to her chin.

"I'm sorry my car isn't larger," Pete said.

"We're fine," Shelby called from the backseat.

When he pulled up in front of the hotel, Pete hopped out to assist the women before the doorman could. He took Shelby's hand. "Thanks for this morning," he said, looking longingly at her.

Shelby stepped forward and gave him a quick kiss on his cheek before stepping back. "Thank you for teaching me."

"We could go again tomorrow morning," he offered before she could walk away.

"Maybe another day," she said, backing toward the hotel.

When they'd entered the lobby, Kay commented, "He seemed disappointed."

"We had fun this morning. Besides, it got him out of work. No wonder he wanted to go again."

"I don't think he's the work-skipping type. I think he just likes being with you."

Shelby shrugged and changed the subject. "What are we going to wear to the party? Maybe we should go shopping this afternoon."

Kay's face brightened. "I'd love to."

After an hour in the hotel shop they each ended up with a dress.

"I think you're going to look smashing, Aunt Kay. Very sexy. Not at all demure, like you usually look."

Shelby added a teasing smile. "That dress makes you look much younger. Maybe twenty-nine instead of thirty-four."

"If it'll knock off five years, I'll definitely wear it." She jabbed the button for the elevator. "Oh, look, Shelby," she said, pointing to a sign in the lobby. "Tonight they have a luau. Do you want to go?"

"You can't come to Hawaii without experiencing an authentic luau. Let's do it."

"Should I call Dan and invite him and Pete? We could treat them for a change."

Kay looked so excited, Shelby couldn't refuse. "If you'd like."

Kay went to the lobby phone and dialed Dan's number. Within a moment she returned. "Dan accepted for him and Pete." Was that disappointment she saw flicker across Shelby's face? No, she convinced herself, Shelby was probably just tired. "You go ahead up. I'll buy the tickets."

"Do you want me to get my share now?"

"No, I'll get it later." Kay didn't intend to, of course. After all, she was the parent. And it was a role she cherished.

After she purchased the tickets, she wandered into one of the lobby shops and bought some chocolate she knew Shelby liked. She could use a quick pick-me-up while she studied.

As Kay rode in the elevator up to their room, she wondered if she'd done the right thing convincing Shelby to come on vacation. Shelby seemed a bit edgy the whole trip. But Kay thought it had been a good thing to get away from the death of her mother and all the hard work of law school.

She wanted Shelby to leave the sadness of her early years completely behind and venture out on a good start in her new life.

Maybe she needed to have a talk with Shelby. After all, they'd always been able to share their feelings. She vividly remembered the hours they'd spent—in Shelby's room when she was younger, then at the kitchen table over coffee—sharing their deepest thoughts or concerns or fears.

Truth be told, Kay missed that on this trip. They'd spent all their time either with the men or apart. Perhaps Shelby missed that, too.

Vowing to rectify that, and looking forward to girl talk and chocolate, Kay stepped into their room.

Chapter Seven

Shelby could only hope Kay would forgive her. Had she done the wrong thing by going along with Dan and his party? Should she warn Kay? No, she didn't think she should do that. Right now her aunt was chattering away happily, munching on chocolate and sipping the drinks Shelby had gotten them. She looked too content to spoil her mood. But the thought of Kay remaining in Hawaii while Shelby returned to Cleveland was too painful.

But, as Dan had said, she couldn't put her own happiness in front of Kay's. Her aunt had made sacrifices for her ten years ago. It was her turn to sacrifice for Kay.

Could she go back to Cleveland without her only family? But how could she stay here?

"Is something wrong?" Kay asked.

"No! I mean, why would you think that?"

"Because you haven't even taken a bite of the chocolate, and it's your favorite."

"I was just thinking about a case I was studying. I was wondering about the laws here in Hawaii. Do you think they differ much from Ohio law?"

"I don't know, honey. Maybe you could buy a book here and find out? Are you thinking of moving to Hawaii?"

Shelby managed a smile. "I was just thinking about how nice it is here."

"Yes, it is, isn't it? Dan's house is magnificent, too."

"Even if I got my law license here, I don't think I could afford a house like that."

"Nor could I. But it's nice to dream about it, isn't it?"

Dan picked up Pete to go to the hotel that evening.

As soon as Pete got settled in the car, he asked, "Have you found an attorney you want to hire for the company?"

"I've got one on retainer. Why? Do we have a lawsuit coming up that I don't know about?"

"No. I just wondered because Shelby said she thought she would prefer working as a corporate attorney instead of a trial attorney."

"Really? I didn't know that."

"I just thought I should mention it." Pete watched Dan's face.

Dan turned to look at him. "What?"

"It might be kind of nice to have your daughter work in your company."

"Nice for me or for you?"

"Aw, Dan, you know what I mean."

"I do. And more than anything, I'd love to get to know Shelby, to spend time with her. But she won't want to stay if we don't find a way to keep Kay here, too. They're a package deal."

"Well, we're off to a good start with the party tomorrow night. Maybe Kay will find someone she's interested in."

Dan's face darkened. "Yeah, maybe."

Pete didn't say anything else until they got to the hotel. He just watched Dan, wondering what had upset him. His guess would be the thought of finding a man for Kay. Pete knew his friend better than anyone. He had to, after spending three-quarters of the day together for the past seven years. Pete would bet the store that Dan was in love with Kay, but maybe he didn't realize it yet.

The biggest problem for his buddy was Shelby. She seemed to think Dan was too old for Kay. But Dan had a young heart. At least it seemed that way to Pete. Maybe he could work on Shelby.

A smile broke out across his face. He liked anything that involved Shelby. Yesterday, when he'd been teaching her to surf, he'd found it difficult to concentrate with her near-naked body against his. He was beginning to realize he wanted Shelby to stay in Hawaii, too, maybe even more than Dan.

When they reached the hotel, Dan went in to call the women. He returned quickly. "Shelby said they'd be right down."

"Good." What else could he say? He certainly couldn't honestly say he was happy to wait. He wanted to see her at once. Was that the way Dan felt about Kay? But could he be as selfless as Dan by letting her go? No, he couldn't. But he might have to.

"Hi, you got here early," Kay said as she and Shelby arrived in the lobby.

Dan gave a casual laugh. "We're always early when we can see you two."

"Oh, you!" Kay exclaimed. "You're always a flirt. It's a wonder some woman hasn't caught you!"

"Several have tried, but I've outfoxed them."

"Come on, we've got a little while before the luau starts. Let's go up to the lounge and have a drink."

"With pleasure," Dan said, taking Kay's hand.

Shelby was just standing there, frowning at them.

"Shelby?" Pete held out a hand to her. "Shall we go?"

"Oh! Oh, yes, of course."

"Something on your mind?"

"No, nothing at all. I'm looking forward to the luau."

"You've never been to one before?" Pete asked without thinking.

She gave him a strange look. "Do you really think we have luaus in Cleveland?"

"I guess not. Sorry, I wasn't thinking when I asked that."

"What were you thinking about?"

"You don't want to know."

"I don't?" Shelby asked as they joined Dan and Kay in the elevator.

"Later," he whispered, hoping the other two wouldn't ask what they were talking about.

When they reached the lounge, Shelby asked for mineral water and Pete echoed her order. She turned to stare at him. "Why did you do that?"

"Because it's what I want, too." He smiled but said nothing else.

Shelby remained silent, but she gave him a strange look.

Dan and Kay each had a glass of wine. They drank it slowly as they talked. Kay was asking Dan about the luau. Like Shelby, she'd never been to one.

"You'll get to try poi," Dan said with a grin.

"Is it good?" Kay asked.

Pete laughed, but Dan said, "Let's just say it's an acquired taste."

"I want to try it," Kay said. "I doubt I'll get back here ever again."

"You never know," Dan said, a touch of sadness in his voice.

"Maybe you can learn to hula, too, Kay," Shelby suggested with a grin.

Kay got a little flustered. "Well, I'm sure I could, but I'm not sure I want to. It's a little...outlandish, isn't it?"

"Probably so," Shelby agreed. "But you're on vacation. What better time to be outlandish?"

"I think I can help you with the hula," Pete said.

"You know how?" Shelby asked in surprise.

"Not exactly, but I dated a hula dancer once."

"And she told you the secret?"

"Sure."

"Maybe you'd better share that little tidbit, Pete," Dan said.

"You mean you don't know?" Kay asked, surprised.

"Not me. I never dated a hula dancer."

"Then I guess Pete can help all of us," Shelby said.

"Whoa!" Dan said. "I didn't say *I* wanted to learn. I just wanted to know the secret. You and Kay are the ones who should learn."

"Chicken," Kay teased.

Dan leaned back and grinned. "We'll wait until you're up on the stage, trying to hula."

Kay's expression turned anxious. "You don't mean they really invite people up on the stage?"

"Of course they do. The customers become the entertainment, and I can't wait for you to join them." Dan rubbed his hands together in exaggerated glee.

"It's okay," Shelby said comfortingly. "Maybe they won't pick you."

"If they do, I'm sure you can do a creditable job," Pete said. "Once I've told you the secret."

"This secret had better be impressive," Shelby muttered.

"It's no big deal. She said you have to remain still with your upper body and think of your hips as loose, able to go from side to side."

Both women stared at him. Finally Shelby said, "Is that all?"

"Well, I've never tried," Pete said.

"I think it would be appropriate to volunteer you, too."

Pete shot an apprehensive look at Shelby. "I don't think they ask men to volunteer."

Kay wagged a finger at him. "After leading us down the rosy path with a promise that isn't worth much, we might make an exception to that rule, young man."

The luau was a fun picnic at the beach. The two women tried everything, even poi. Kay decided it wasn't bad, though she thought it would taste better if it didn't look like gray paste.

Just as they were completely relaxed, a beautiful young Hawaiian native came onto the outdoor stage to show the crowd the hula and explain the significance of its movements.

Kay and Shelby were entranced and hung on the young woman's every word. Then the dancer invited onstage anyone who wanted to learn to hula.

Kay and Shelby looked at each other, then they got up and went onstage. Once there, Shelby whispered to the young woman. About ten women had volunteered, but that wasn't enough for Shelby. The woman stepped to the microphone and said, "We've had a special request for Mr. Pete Campbell to join us onstage."

Pete sat there in frozen horror. Dan, after one look at his young friend, pointed to Pete for the hostess. It took some persuading but Pete finally joined the women.

"I'll get you for this, Shelby," Pete promised.

Shelby gave him a contented smile. "You mean you'll show me up?"

"No, that's not what I mean," he growled.

The dancer gave them instructions and then turned to face the audience. Pete, though, couldn't keep his eyes off Shelby. They'd put grass skirts on all the women, and he found the swishing sound mesmerizing as she swayed her hips. The same hips he'd held on the surfboard.

Then the dancer called to him. "You need to come up here with me."

He stood stock-still, hoping he'd misheard. However, she was rolling her finger for him to come forward. After throwing a desperate look at Shelby, he went up to the dancer.

"I think you need some special instruction," the woman said and moved behind him, putting her hands on his hips. Pete thought he was going to pass out. Until he saw Dan rolling on the grass, laughing hysterically. He decided he'd show Dan, and Shelby, too, that he could hula as well as anyone.

"Good job, Pete," the dancer said as they ended the amateur demonstration. "You did better than I thought you would."

"Thanks," he said as Shelby approached, hoping she'd heard the woman's words.

Shelby agreed. "I guess he does know the secret of hula dancing."

Pete grabbed her hand and walked offstage with her. However, he didn't say anything until they reached the table. "I think you owe me an apology, Dan."

"You're right, I do," Dan said with a grin. "In fact, I

even doubted the ladies could hula, but you were all great—the best ones onstage."

"Thank you," Pete said with dignity.

The entertainment turned serious when native dancers twirled rings of fire and knives. Shelby leaned toward Pete. "Good thing they didn't ask for volunteers for this dance."

"Yeah. I don't dance as well with sharp knives or fire."

Shelby chuckled. "Me, neither." After a moment of companionable silence, she leaned close again. "Have you forgiven me?"

"Not yet. I think it may take a few kisses for me to forgive you."

"Oh, my. I had no idea I offended you that much."

"I warned you," he said with a grin.

"Maybe I could just make a down payment and pay it out?"

He frowned. "That's not what I'd planned."

"So we're going to kiss in front of Dan and Kay?"

"I was thinking we could take a walk on the beach in the moonlight. They always end these things with general dancing or a singer. I thought we could go then."

"Maybe. I'd have to see if Kay is all right with that."

"Shelby, you're not a child. You don't have to ask permission."

"No, but I need to know that Kay will be all right."

Pete shook his head. "She's an adult, too."

"Well, how about I don't ask her? Will that suit you?"

As he nodded, a smile on his face, she added, "Then that means I won't be leaving Kay's side. Happy now?"

Pete made a disgusted sound. "Okay, do what you want."

About that time, they introduced a singer. Shelby leaned over and whispered something to Kay. Then she stood. When Pete didn't move, she said, "Aren't you coming?"

Pete scrambled to his feet and grabbed her hand. "Yeah, I'm coming."

"What was that all about?" Dan asked as he saw Pete and Shelby walking away.

"They're going for a walk on the beach. She told me there was no need to wait for her. She had her key and would come up when she was ready."

"She thought the old folks couldn't stay up long enough?" Dan asked, sarcasm in his voice.

"You're being silly, Dan. Shelby doesn't think of us as old people. She just wanted to let me know I was able to do what I wanted without worrying about her."

"So, you can do what you want?"

"Why, yes, I suppose, if there's something I want to do."

"I think a stroll on the beach would be nice."

"I guess we could do that, as long as we went in the opposite direction of those two."

"If you get too excited, you're going to make me not want to go," Dan said, using sarcasm again.

Kay tried to hold back a smile, but she couldn't.

"I promise to be more interested once we're alone on the beach."

"Well now, that sounds promising," Dan said, wiggling his brows at her.

"The beach is so beautiful in the moonlight," Shelby said with a sigh, walking with her hand in Pete's.

"It's not half as beautiful as you."

"Oh, Pete, you're exaggerating, but I appreciate it."

"When you wear you hair down, you make me want to hold you and never let you go."

Though she was thrilled, Shelby's happiness was tainted by a touch of sadness. "But you can't, Pete. I'm going back to Cleveland. All I'll be able to take home with me are the wonderful memories I'll have."

"Then, come here, sweetheart, and let's make a few more memories." He pulled her into the shadows of a palm tree.

"I want to talk to you about Shelby," Kay said as she walked onto the beach with Dan.

He reached out and took her hand. "So, do we know which way the young 'uns went?" he asked in an exaggerated drawl.

"I think they went that-a-way," Kay said in a hoarse whisper.

Dan tightened his hold on Kay's hand. "Then we'll go this-a-way!"

They set off on an easy walk, not talking at first. Then Kay said, "I need to know what you want Shelby to do."

"Do about what?"

"About her staying or going."

"I think Shelby is going to do what you do, sweet-heart. She's very devoted to you. Why do you ask?"

"She asked me today if I knew how much difference there was in preparing for the bar exam here or in Ohio."

"How did you answer?"

"I told her I didn't know, but perhaps she could find a book that would show her."

Dan leaned over and kissed Kay's forehead. "Perfect answer."

"It was the truth. I don't know if you want me to encourage her to remain in Hawaii."

"Could you go back to Cleveland without her? That would be pretty drastic, wouldn't it?"

"Yes, it would, but if she wanted to stay with you, I could understand. I certainly wouldn't hold on to her. She's all grown-up now, and I think she really likes Pete, even if she didn't start out that way."

"But you'd be very lonely if you went back without her."

"Of course I would miss her, but…I do have friends."

"Really? Can you name any of them?"

She swung around to stare at him, outrage on her face. "I beg your pardon! I don't think I have to name my friends for you to believe me!"

"No, of course not. But I have a better idea. Why don't you stay here with Shelby? Maybe you'll meet some nice man, marry and have children and you can teach them how to hula."

"Don't be ridiculous!" Kay pulled her hand away and started marching down the beach.

* * *

"Pete," Shelby whispered as his lips traced kisses down her neck, "I don't think we should do this. We don't want to have any regrets when we…we say good-bye."

"How could I regret your sweet kisses, honey? But I have a better idea. I think you should stay here."

"I can't abandon Kay. She's my only family now. I won't leave her alone."

He tilted her chin up. "What if tomorrow night she meets someone she likes? What would happen then?"

"I don't know. We could extend our stay a few days so she could be sure, but it's not a lot of time to make such a life-altering decision."

"I don't know. I think I could make that decision," Pete said.

"You're being silly, Pete. I'm sure you've dated a lot of women, but that doesn't mean you know who you want to live the rest of your life with in one week."

"You don't believe in love at first sight?" he demanded.

"No, and neither do you. Remember? I heard what you thought about me that first night."

"I just didn't think you were friendly. You didn't hear me say you were unattractive, did you?" he challenged.

"I don't think my looks mattered that much to you."

"You're right. They didn't. Because it takes a total package to capture my heart. But it didn't take me long to find out that you had that total package. You're smart, warm, loving, loyal and a hell of a kisser. So come back here and show me again." He pulled her back into his arms and met her lips again.

"Now, honey, don't get upset," Dan pleaded. "I just want you to be happy, too. You deserve it. Like Shelby said, you could marry and have several children. And you'd be a great mother."

"I appreciate the sentiment," she said slowly, having come to a halt. "But I'm an adult. It's not like I run into unmarried men all the time. If I find the right one, I'll marry. If not, I'll continue on with my business."

"Okay, I can agree with that. But you'll keep an open mind, right?"

"Of course." But her mind apparently cut off that topic as she blurted, "Have you ever seen the whales here?"

It took Dan a minute to follow her. "Uh, yeah, I have, but not on the beach. I've gone out on some whale-watching boats. I'd offer to take you, but it's not whale season."

"Too bad. I'd love to see them."

They walked a little farther and Dan asked, "Are we through talking about Shelby?"

"Yes, I think so, as long as Pete is a nice man and would treat Shelby right if they fell in love."

"He is. I've been spending time with him since he was sixteen. I was his Big Brother. I mean, in the Big Brother program."

"Really? I didn't know that."

"I can't guarantee that he'll fall in love with Shelby,

though I think she's beautiful and bright, but that's because she's my daughter."

"No, because I think the same thing."

"But you're her aunt, so neither of us is trustworthy as an impartial judge. But I think he's becoming more and more interested."

"Then maybe something exciting will happen. Still, two weeks doesn't seem quite enough time."

"You don't think so?" Dan asked. "Then I've got the perfect solution. The two of you can move into my house when your hotel reservation runs out."

"We can't do that, Dan. What would people think?"

"That I'm a damn lucky guy."

She tilted her head up to share her smile with him. "Shame on you. Teasing as usual."

Maybe it was the way the moonlight lit up her face. Or how her smile reached her eyes. Dan didn't know exactly why, but at that moment he felt poleaxed by Kay. Suddenly the desire to fold her in his arms and kiss her was almost overwhelming.

Dan knew he was in trouble.

Big trouble.

Chapter Eight

"I think it's time to go back. Let's go find the other two."

Kay didn't know what happened, but Dan suddenly turned away from her and began moving down the beach at a rapid rate.

"I don't think Shelby wants me to check on her," Kay called after him. She sped up to join him. What had gotten into him? "Dan, why are we running?"

"I...I think it might rain. You know, when you get old you can feel it in your joints."

Kay frowned, but she didn't offer any more protests. It wasn't easy to stay even with Dan, but he took her hand in his and tugged her along.

They passed the luau area and continued, only pausing to look closely at several couples along the way. They almost passed by a couple tightly wound in each other's embrace, kissing.

Dan came to an abrupt halt. "Pete!"

When there was no response, he stepped closer and called again.

Pete raised his head slowly and looked at Dan. Then, as if the sight of him had released him from the trance he was in, he jumped away from Shelby. "Dan! What are you doing here?"

"It's time to go. Come on."

Pete came closer, but he'd taken Shelby by her hand and brought her with him. "What's wrong, Dan?"

"Nothing. It's time to go home."

Shelby looked at Kay, who shrugged her shoulders.

"Is there a problem, Dan?" Shelby asked.

"Yeah. I have to go home to get ready for tomorrow. Pete, I need you to come with me."

"Uh, yeah, sure, Dan. I'll just, uh, tell Shelby goodbye and be with you in a minute."

It was clear to Dan that Pete's goodbye to Shelby would take more time than Dan could handle. "No, I think you've already told her goodbye. Come on."

Pete looked into Dan's intense gaze and decided he was right. He leaned over and dropped a quick kiss on Shelby's swollen lips. Then he crossed the sand to Dan. "Okay."

"We'll see you two ladies tomorrow night," Dan said before they both turned and walked back toward the hotel parking lot.

Shelby crossed to Kay. "Did you and Dan have an argument?"

"If we did, I didn't know about it. Dan suddenly decided he couldn't be here any longer, but I have no idea why."

"Do you think we're still invited for tomorrow night?"

"He just said so, but we'll call tomorrow after he leaves for work and speak to Betty. I don't think I want to discuss anything with Dan right now."

"Okay. I guess we'll have an early evening after all."

They headed back to their hotel room. Then Kay paused to look at the dark sky. "Do you think it looks like rain?"

"What was that all about?" Pete demanded. "I didn't think you minded if I, uh, dated Shelby."

"I don't if Shelby doesn't," Dan growled.

"Then if it wasn't me kissing Shelby, what's wrong?"

"It was me kissing Kay," Dan snapped.

Pete stared at his friend and mentor, his mouth open.

"Close your mouth before a fly gets in."

"But I didn't know— That is, do you— Damn it, Dan, you didn't tell me you were in love with Kay!"

"I'm not!" Realizing he'd overreacted, Dan cleared his throat. "You don't have to be in love to want to kiss someone. She looked up at me, laughing in the moonlight, and...it was just an impulse, but I knew— I didn't want to mess things up for tomorrow night. She might get the wrong idea."

"Okay," Pete said, drawing out the word. "So you don't have any problem with me and Shelby?"

"No, but she might not stay here. Especially when I tell her the truth."

"Does she have to know?"

"You would have me lie to my own child?"

"Isn't that what you've been doing for twenty years? Why change now?"

Anger built in Dan. "You don't mean that! But if you do, don't tell me! I'm going to tell her. Just not until the right moment."

They rode in silence until they reached Dan's house. When Pete reached for the car door handle, Dan stopped him. "Pete, you understand that I have to tell her, don't you?"

"Yeah, I do, Dan. Sorry I made such a bonehead response. I don't even know if I'm serious about Shelby, but I know I'd like her to stay longer."

"For someone not serious, you sure were busy on the beach."

"Come on, Dan, you're not that old."

"Yeah, but we're talking about my daughter!"

"Who, believe me, is quite capable of saying no. She can take care of herself. That's one of the things I like about her. She's strong, independent."

"Yes. And very protective of her aunt." Dan sighed. "Okay, I'll see you in the morning."

"Yeah. Thanks for the ride."

Dan watched as Pete drove away. It had been an interesting night. He had a lot of thinking to do.

* * *

Shelby and Kay arrived at the Jackson house at three, as they had promised Betty. Kay breathed a sigh of relief when the housekeeper answered the door.

"Come in. It's so nice of you to offer to help me. Let's take your things to one of the bedrooms." Betty turned and led them down the hall to a lovely, quiet bedroom. "There's a bath through that door. You can come here to change for the party."

"This is lovely, Betty," Shelby said with a smile. She put her things down, hanging her dress in a closet nearby. "But now we're ready to work. Lead the way."

Betty led them to the huge kitchen at the other end of the house. Kay stood mesmerized by the expanse and cool efficiency of the room. From almost anywhere in the room was a panoramic view of the sun-kissed ocean. "My heavens, this is such a beautiful kitchen. I thought I'd imagined it."

Betty beamed with pride.

Shelby moved past her aunt. "What can we do to help?"

Betty assigned each of them jobs, and they pitched in and did every chore she gave them.

"You two are wonderful. Once, Mr. Dan had a woman here who insisted she wanted to help, but all she did was put on a frilly apron and give orders. She almost drove me crazy."

Kay looked at Betty. "I guess Dan often has women guests. After all, he's very handsome."

"Not all that much. Unless it's for business, he

doesn't entertain much. Pete hangs out here a lot, and a few other friends, but not many women."

Kay nodded, and Shelby thought she looked pleased. Once again, Shelby wondered what her aunt's relationship with Dan was about. Shelby still thought he was too old for Kay. Perhaps tonight she'd meet someone who'd interest her. And what would Shelby do if her aunt decided to stay in Hawaii?

Shelby didn't know.

"Guests will start arriving in half an hour. You two need to go change," Betty said, shooing them out of the kitchen. "You've done so much work, there's almost nothing left for me to do. Thank you."

They started for the bedroom they'd been assigned at the other end of the house, when Dan suddenly appeared in front of them.

"I hope you ladies didn't work too hard in the kitchen."

Kay, Shelby noticed, averted her glance and remained silent, so Shelby answered. "Not at all. Betty was fun to work with. I learned a few things from her."

"Yes, she's very good. Kay, did you enjoy yourself?"

"Yes, I did." She started to move down the hall. "We're going to get dressed now."

Dan stepped aside. "Of course, I don't want to hold you up."

After they reached the room, Shelby asked, "Are you mad at Dan?"

"Not really, but last night he seemed… Oh, I don't know, a little distant. I don't want him to think we're taking advantage of him."

"How could he? We didn't plan a party and invite him. He's the host. Plus, we volunteered to help Betty. And we really did help."

"Yes, we did, didn't we?" Kay finally smiled.

"Come on, let's get dressed. We don't want to be late for the party."

When they slipped into their new dresses, Shelby grew even more concerned for her aunt. Kay had no idea how sexy she looked in her black sundress. The neckline hinted at cleavage; the cinched waistline showed off her best asset. With her blond hair and gentle smile, Kay would be a magnet for every man in the room.

Shelby knew she'd better keep a close eye on Kay. The woman was relatively inexperienced with men.

Shelby laughed to herself. As if she herself was an expert! But between the two of them they'd cope with the different types of men tonight.

When they emerged from the bedroom, there were already several guests in the living room. Dan came immediately to introduce them. As they all settled down, Shelby slipped into the kitchen to see if Betty needed any more help.

"Betty, I—" She stopped when she saw Pete. He looked up at her and with one glance her mouth went dry. She managed, "I didn't know you'd arrived. What are you doing in the kitchen?"

Pete grinned. "I had to say hello to Betty. She's my favorite girl."

Betty rolled her eyes. "Only when you're hungry."

Shelby laughed. "I can believe that. I came to see if there was something I could do."

"Yes, there is. Each of you can take one of these platters out and then go have fun."

"Okay." Shelby picked up one and Pete the other and headed for the living room.

They were greeted warmly by the growing number of guests.

"Betty's reputation must be widespread," Shelby said to Pete.

"You'd better believe it. That's why Dan's parties are always well attended." He leaned in close and whispered, "Want to take a stroll on the patio? I think I can find some secluded place where no one would see me kiss you."

Shelby ignored what just the promise of Pete's kiss did to her. She had a job to do tonight. "I can't. I have to keep an eye on Kay. She might need some help."

"Dan's watching her like a hawk. Why do you have to?"

"Because I don't want her to be embarrassed or upset."

Pete didn't look happy. "Okay, if we have to stay inside, let me introduce you to the lawyer Dan has on retainer. You can discuss lawyer things."

Though Pete sounded terribly uninterested in "lawyer things," he stayed by Shelby's side after introducing her to Angus Wynn, the elderly lawyer working for Dan.

And it was Pete who suggested Angus tell Shelby the

differences between preparing for the bar exam here and in, say, Ohio.

Before that discussion could progress beyond generalities, several other guests joined their group and the conversation drifted into other areas.

Pete seemed upset with the other guests. When Shelby whispered, "What's wrong?" Pete answered, "You're being surrounded by men. Didn't you notice?"

Shelby looked up, surprised. She hadn't realized the only people around her were men. She smiled at all of them and said, "Excuse me. I need to see if Betty needs any help."

She headed for the kitchen, after glancing at Kay, who was laughing at something one of the men around her had said. She was surprised to find Pete following her. "Where are you going?"

"To the kitchen with you," he replied with a smile. "I know a way out of the kitchen onto the patio. We can—"

"No, I told you I have to—"

"—keep an eye on Kay," Pete finished for her. "I know all about that."

Shelby stood straighter and raised her chin. "I think she needs my help."

"And I think she's a convenient excuse." When Shelby gasped at his remark, he said, "If you don't want to go outside with me, why don't you just tell me?"

"Fine! I don't want to go outside with you."

"Fine!" Pete returned and stomped out of the kitchen.

As if reading her mind, Betty said, "My, my. I haven't seen Pete that angry in a long time."

Why was Pete being so pigheaded? Shelby thought. Couldn't he see she had to sacrifice her own desires tonight and be there for her aunt? After all, this party was for Kay. Still, Pete was seriously angry... Later on she'd find a minute to talk to him.

"I'm sorry to have an argument in your kitchen, Betty. I just wanted to see if you needed any help."

"Well, since you asked, could you carry out this big tray? I have some things on the stove."

"I'd be glad to." Shelby picked up the tray and headed for the living room, where she deposited it on the bar. There was no sign of Pete.

"Is everything okay in the kitchen?" Dan whispered as he came alongside her.

Had he heard? Summoning her composure, she played it cool. "Yes, of course. What about out here?" Her gaze strayed to Kay, who was now seated between two men on one of the couches.

Dan's reply assured her all was well, but his body language said differently.

"Why do you look so unhappy?"

"I'm not," Dan immediately assured her before turning away to speak to one of his guests. But Shelby noticed he didn't stray far from Kay's side.

Angus, she noticed, was alone now, so she joined him and continued their interrupted discussion.

Dan was leaning against the bar, keeping an eye on Kay, when he was joined by Pete. "What are you doing?" he asked.

"What do you mean? I'm...I'm here to sample whatever Betty has on this tray," Pete said, picking up a stuffed mushroom cap.

"So it's hunger that drove you over here?"

"Yeah, of course."

"Where's Shelby?" Dan asked.

"I'm not her keeper!" Pete growled.

"Uh-oh, trouble in paradise?"

"Of course not! She just didn't want— She thinks she has to keep an eye on Kay. I told her you were doing a great job of that, but she still thinks she should take care of her."

"I'm sure Kay can take care of herself."

"So why are you watching her?"

Dan sighed. "It's kind of like watching a car wreck. You know you shouldn't be so interested, but you can't help yourself."

"A car wreck? Why would you say that, Dan?"

"Never mind. I'm not thinking straight tonight."

Suddenly he noticed Kay had excused herself and was heading for the kitchen. He hurried after, leaving Pete standing at the bar.

"Kay? Is something wrong? Did someone get fresh?" Dan demanded as he came through the door, interrupting a quiet conversation between Kay and Betty.

Kay turned to stare at Dan. "What are you talking about? Of course not. How ridiculous!"

"Then what's wrong?"

"Nothing's wrong as far as I know," Kay said. "You're the one who came rushing in. You tell me!"

"No, nothing's— I just thought— Are you having fun?" he finally asked.

With a smile she quickly hid, Betty turned back to her cooking while Kay continued to stare at Dan as if trying to figure him out. He felt like such a fool.

"Am I having fun? That's what was so important? Then, yes, Dan, the evening is very nice."

"But are you meeting anyone you…like?"

With a puzzled look, Kay said, "Of course. Your friends are very interesting."

"Damn it! That's not what—" He stopped himself before he revealed too much. "Yes, of course. Shall we rejoin them?"

After a quick look over her shoulder to Betty, Kay moved toward Dan. "Of course, if that's what you want."

"Well, I certainly don't want you to hide in the kitchen."

"I wasn't hiding," Kay said sternly. "I wanted to see if Betty needed more help."

"She'll manage. Right, Betty?"

"Of course, Mr. Dan."

"See? Now let's get back to the party."

Kay and Shelby didn't get back to their hotel room till midnight. They both collapsed upon their respective beds as soon as they entered the room.

"Are you as tired as I am?" Kay asked, reluctant to move, even to undress.

"Yes. It was a nice party, but—"

"I know. Not knowing anyone except for Dan and Pete made it hard work, didn't it?"

"Yes, it did. Did you meet Angus Wynn? I enjoyed talking to him about the laws here in Hawaii."

"Yes, I met him. He's very nice, but I think he's a little old for you."

She laughed. "I think he's even old for Methuselah."

"Where was Pete tonight? I didn't see much of him."

"Oh, he got too demanding. When I refused to—" She couldn't tell Kay about her chaperone assignment. "He got angry and refused to speak to me anymore."

"How silly of him," Kay said with a smile. "Men can get rather possessive sometimes."

"Aunt Kay, did you ever— I mean, I don't remember any particular boyfriend after I came to live with you. I guess I should've asked before now, but…did I ruin your life?"

"No, sweetheart, you didn't. I think you made my life perfect."

Shelby sat up on her bed. "But you could've married and had children, your own family."

"But you've told me it's not too late, right?"

"Right. That's why—" Shelby stopped herself.

After a moment of silence, Kay said, "That's why what?"

Shelby searched her aunt's eyes and knew from their expression she was caught. She should've known better than to think she could hide anything from this woman. Especially something like this.

"That's why Dan wanted to have the party, to introduce you to men young enough for you to marry and have a family with."

Kay jumped off the bed. "What? And you went along with it?"

"I want you to be happy!" Shelby exclaimed, begging with her gaze for Kay to understand.

"That was the purpose of the party?"

"Yes," Shelby whispered.

"And what were you going to do if I found someone here in Hawaii to marry? Were you going to stay?"

"I don't know."

Tears welled up in Kay's eyes and spilled down her cheeks. She hung her head and sighed. Shelby couldn't remember the last time she'd seen her aunt cry. Not even at Cordelia's funeral.

"What is it, Aunt Kay?"

"Oh, Shelby, I should never have lied to you. But I thought I was helping you. I think it's about time I told you the truth."

Chapter Nine

Chills ran up her spine, and a knot formed in her stomach as Shelby saw Kay's tortured expression. She wanted her aunt to tell her the truth, yet at the same time she was almost afraid to hear it.

Kay reached out to her. "Honey, please remember that I thought it was best for you."

"What is it, Aunt Kay?"

"Do you remember all the horrible things your mother told you about your father?"

Shelby drew away from her aunt, wrapping her arms around herself. "Yes," she whispered.

"Well, they were all lies, concocted by my sister to make you hate him."

"How do you know?"

"Because I was there. Remember, I lived with you and Cordelia until I went to college. I was there when you were little, when your father came to see you, and Cordy had scared you so badly, it was as if he were the bogeyman."

Shelby stared at her but said nothing else.

"Your father was a good man."

A good man? Shelby doubted so. He'd left her. She said as much to Kay.

"He left because I begged him to," Kay explained.

"Why would you do that?"

"Because your mother was going to ruin your life, filling it with hate for your father. She got hysterical every time he even called, then took it out on you. I was afraid for you. And for your father. He loved you very much. But the courts back then favored the mother, and he didn't have any money to fight her."

Kay wiped away the tears that continued to slide down her cheeks. "So I sent him away and promised I'd take care of you."

"You kept your word," Shelby said, on the verge of tears herself.

"Yes, but I don't think I was right."

Shelby searched her aunt's gaze and found pain and regret hidden in their blue depths. "Kay, what—"

"Let me finish, Shelby. I feared if your father returned before your mother was dead, there would be a nasty fight and…I envisioned it ending in tragedy."

"I'm sure you were right, Kay. Mom never said a

good word about my father. But what does that have to do with your lying to me?"

"Oh, dear, this is harder than I thought it would be." Kay buried her face in her hands. Then she raised her head and took a deep breath. "Dan is your father."

What did she say? Shelby stared at Kay, unable to process her words. Dan? She'd pictured her father as a little girl, and he'd looked like an evil man. She guessed that wasn't surprising, since her mother had told her so many terrible things about him.

Kay was telling her Dan was her father? Dan Jackson, the man she'd met a few days ago?

Somehow, that idea had trouble catching hold. "That…that can't be true! He left me with Mom and—"

"I know, Shelby. I begged him to. I wrote him letters and sent pictures, but I denied him your childhood and I denied you the right to know your father. I wasn't an adult, but I couldn't stand to see you both suffering. I thought it would be better if he went away." On a sob she asked, "Shelby, can you ever forgive me?"

Kay had raised her, shared everything with her, gotten her through the rough times. But right now Shelby stared at her beloved aunt as if she were a total stranger. "I…I don't know what to say."

Kay took her hand. "I'll tell you anything you want to know."

"Why didn't he come back after I moved in with you? Didn't he care?" Scores of questions bombarded her.

"That was my fault. I wanted you to stay in contact

with Cordy. I knew she needed you. You were all that stood between her and destruction. So I begged Dan to wait awhile."

Suddenly it was all too much for Shelby. Her mind was reeling, her head pounding. She pulled her hand back and got up from her bed, almost staggering to the lanai door. "I need to be alone."

On the lanai she leaned against the rail, drawing in deep gulps of air. The sounds of the surf did nothing to soothe her now.

It frightened Shelby to think that Aunt Kay—her beloved aunt—had lied to her. Had persuaded her into a vacation, when, in reality, she was bringing her to meet that most-hated figure—her father.

She'd hoped for someone to rescue her from her home, from her mother and her hated stepfather. And Kay *had* rescued her. All those years suffering with her mother, when she could've been with a father who loved her and wanted her. But she hadn't known that person existed.

It had been like walking on eggshells in her home. Her mother had been erratic and sometimes violent. Shelby had learned at an early age to disappear when Cordelia reached a certain level of frustration or anger.

Though she hated her stepfather, her life had been easier after her mother's second marriage because her anger was more focused on her husband than it was on her child. But he'd never been a father figure to Shelby.

She didn't really know what a father was supposed to be. She'd looked longingly at other little girls playing with their daddies, or being carried in their father's strong arms. She'd wondered what was wrong with her that she couldn't have a daddy.

Once, she'd asked Aunt Kay if she was the reason her father had left. Somehow he seemed to hold the key to something in her life, but she didn't even know what. After a while with Aunt Kay, a supportive, loving mother figure, Shelby had put aside her longings for she knew not what and surged ahead with her life.

Now those longings came back fourfold. Kay had known about her father. She remembered, now, Kay cautioning her about believing everything her mother said.

Dan. Dan was her father. Kind, gentle Dan. Strong, yet friendly Dan. Dan, who hadn't spoken up about his fatherhood.

Maybe he still didn't want her.

That thought brought her to another point. Why had he wanted to find Kay a husband here in Hawaii? Was it because he knew Shelby wouldn't stay here without Kay? Because she wouldn't. She owed Kay too much.

Did Pete know? Yes, she thought, he must. He'd acted almost jealous tonight. Because he thought he had a chance with the boss's daughter? How dare he!

Shelby pushed off the rail and went back into the hotel room.

Without preamble she asked, "Kay, does Pete know? Is that why he's been hanging around, hoping to marry the boss's daughter?"

Kay, who'd been lying down, still crying quietly, sprang

up to a sitting position on the bed. "I don't know, Shelby, but I'm sure his interest has nothing to do with Dan."

"I think that's why Dan was trying to find you a husband tonight. He knows I won't stay here without you."

Kay held up a hand. "I'd rather not rehash that."

"I'm sorry." She sat down beside her and wiped her aunt's tears with the palm of her hand. "Oh, Kay, what are we going to do?"

"About what? Don't you want to be with Dan?"

"Why would I? He hasn't declared himself as my father. No, you and I came together and we'll go together. If he ever admits he's my father, I'll maintain contact with him by letter, like you did, but I'm not staying here without you."

"Shelby, he wants to make up for lost time. You shouldn't blame him. I'm the one who sent him away. He even sent me child support while you were living with me. He paid for your college and law school. It's my fault that you didn't know about his support. Blame me, honey."

Shelby gazed at Kay, the woman she regarded more dearly than anyone on earth. How could she ever blame Kay for anything? She reached out and hugged her in a warm embrace. "I can't blame you, Kay. You're the one who protected me, gave me hope. Maybe Dan did some nice things for me and I'll thank him, I suppose, but that doesn't mean I'll stay here while you return to Cleveland. And I don't intend to give him, or Pete, the opportunity to try to convince me otherwise."

"What do you mean? Are you going back home early?"

"No, I refuse to let them ruin my vacation. But there are plenty other places on the island we can go without them. Will you go with me, Kay?"

Her aunt smiled at her. "Haven't I always?"

His body may have been there, behind the oval-shaped teak desk at Island Traders, but Dan's mind was somewhere else. Like last night, he had a hard time concentrating on anything other than Kay. Had she met anyone at the party she was interested in? Dan worried that she had. He worried that she hadn't.

He was a mess.

Somewhere around daybreak, after a sleepless night, he'd come to that realization. As well as another one.

He was in love with the young woman who had saved his daughter.

But as Shelby herself had told him, he was too old for Kay. So he'd done his best to help her find happiness by inviting every single, eligible, successful man he knew to the party last night.

And now he could hit himself for it. What if she'd fallen for one of them?

Eyeing the stacks of paperwork and a new contract on his desk, Dan forced himself to focus. But little was accomplished. His secretary caught him several times staring out into space. When the door opened again close to noon, he immediately started shuffling papers so he'd look busy. But it wasn't his secretary.

Pete entered his office. "Dan, have you talked to the girls?"

"You mean Kay and Shelby?"

"Of course I mean them. Who else would I mean?" Clearly, Pete was not in a good mood, either.

"No, I haven't talked to them."

"I thought you would've been anxious to talk to Kay, to see how she felt about the men she met last night."

If Pete only knew…. "I thought they might sleep late. I was going to call in a minute to see if they wanted to go out for lunch."

"Don't bother. They haven't answered their phone all morning."

"How early did you call?"

"Nine o'clock. Shelby and I had some problems last night. I wanted to clear the air."

"Maybe they were at breakfast," Dan said, frowning.

"Maybe."

"Did you leave a message?"

"Not the first time. But I did the second time. And the third. And the fourth."

"And she never called you back? Maybe Shelby is mad at you. I'll call Kay." Dan picked up his phone and called the hotel, asking for Kay's room.

After ten rings the phone switched to voice mail. "I was hoping to take you to lunch today," Dan said, "but I guess you're already out. We'll plan on dinner. Call me when you get in."

Pete stood by the desk, his arms crossed. "And if she doesn't call?"

"If I haven't heard from her by the end of the workday, I'll call again."

"Let me know what you hear," Pete growled, and stomped out of the office.

Now Dan had even more to think about. His day was wasted.

He hadn't heard from Kay when it was time to leave at five. He tried the hotel again with the same results. Wearily, he packed up his laptop and got ready to leave. As he did so, his office door opened again.

"Did you hear from them?" From his tone, Pete's mood hadn't improved.

Dan shook his head. "Did you?"

"No. Do you think they're intentionally avoiding us?"

"I don't think Kay would do that. Kay's been enthusiastic about me getting to know Shelby. Why would that change?"

"I don't know. But I don't like this."

Neither did he. "Why don't you come home with me for dinner? We'll see what we can do. They'll probably be at the hotel soon."

"Do you think Betty will mind?"

"Does she ever?"

Pete turned and called over his shoulder as he exited, "Thanks. I'll see you there."

Dan called home to tell Betty about the dinner guest.

"Of course, Mr. Dan." He could practically hear her smile. Betty loved when Pete ate with them. He always lavished her with compliments. "Oh, I almost forgot. The ladies came by this morning and left a note for you."

"Why didn't you call me?"

"They said it was a thank-you for last night, so I didn't—"

"Get the note and read it to me, please."

Betty came back to the phone quickly. "It says, 'Thank you for the party last evening. That was kind of you. Shelby and I are going to do some sightseeing now. We'll call you before we leave. Thanks again for your hospitality. Kay.'"

Dan couldn't speak. He was too busy trying to decipher the hidden meaning of Kay's words.

"Is something wrong?" Betty prompted.

"Yeah, I think so. Thanks, Betty. Pete and I will be there soon."

Pete entered moments after Dan, discovering his friend sitting on the sofa with a white card in his hand.

"What's that?"

Without looking up, Dan replied, "A card Kay and Shelby dropped off earlier today."

"I gather it doesn't contain good news."

"I don't think so, though she doesn't say anything bad."

Dan gave the note to Pete, who, after reading it, collapsed on the sofa beside him. "That's a sweet goodbye note if ever I read one."

"My thoughts exactly."

Betty came in and stood there as if studying the despondent pair. "Are you ready to eat dinner?"

Neither of them answered.

"What's wrong?" she asked anxiously.

Dan looked up. "It seems the ladies have tired of our company."

"They were very pleasant when they stopped by this morning."

"Did they say where they were going?" Pete asked.

"They didn't." Betty forced a cheery smile and coaxed them to the dining table. "I've made your favorite, Mr. Dan."

Neither man ate much of the grilled mahi-mahi.

"What are we going to do?" Pete finally asked. "We can't allow them to just dismiss us, can we?"

"No, of course not. But I'm not sure what to do."

"We could go to the hotel and wait for them."

"And where would we wait? That hotel has three or four entrances."

"You're right. Maybe we go over later and knock on their door."

"Do you think they'd answer?"

"What do we have to lose? An hour of our time that we could spend sitting here staring into space."

"Good point. Let's go."

They started out the door with Dan calling over his shoulder to Betty.

Betty just shook her head. "I've got a feeling those ladies are making them suffer."

"I'm exhausted," Shelby complained as she fell across her bed.

"Me, too. Want to order room service for dinner? I

think it would be a good idea, especially if we want to avoid the guys."

The notion tugged at Shelby's heart. As much as she wanted to be mad at Pete, it hurt her not to see him. But it hurt her more that he'd deceived her.

"Do you think they'll try to contact us after our note?" Kay asked.

"From my experience, men don't take rejection well." Her "experience" consisted of two relationships, both of which ended after a month.

"We told Dan we'd call him before we left," Kay said hesitantly.

"I don't think that will satisfy him. Or Pete. After all, Pete must've thought he'd found the mother lode. The boss's only daughter. He won't give up easily." Shelby sat up and looked on the lamp table between the beds. "No menu here. Is it over on the TV cabinet?"

"Yes, I think so." Kay went to look. "You know, I'm not very hungry."

"You scarcely ate any lunch, Kay. You have to keep your strength up. You can't afford to lose any weight."

"You didn't eat much, either. I guess today wasn't as much fun without the guys."

"Do you just want to go home, then?" Shelby asked. "Because I don't think we can continue with the guys. Not when we know what they're up to."

"Why not? We don't have to let them know we know what they know. Why can't we enjoy their escort?"

"I guess I could withstand Pete's intentions as long as we stay together. And Dan isn't courting you, so—"

"No, he's not," Kay agreed sadly.

"Kay, you act as if you'd like him to." Shelby drew a deep breath. "Are you attracted to Dan? But he's too old for you. That's what I told him."

"Why did you tell him that?"

"I don't remember. I just said you needed someone closer to your own age."

Kay shrugged. "I knew he had no interest in me. I suspect no one could force him to marry into our family again."

Shelby hugged her aunt. "I'm sorry. I really thought he was too old for you."

"I don't suppose it matters. But if you think you can keep Pete in line, I'd enjoy seeing Dan a little more."

Shelby stood, wrapping her arms around her body, and paced across the room. "I guess I could handle Pete. It's only for another week."

"Then—" Kay began, only to be interrupted by a knock on their door.

"Could it be them?" Kay whispered.

Shelby tiptoed to the door to peer through the peephole. She turned and silently questioned Kay.

She nodded. "Open it."

Shelby did as Kay had asked, but she wasn't sure it was a wise move. When she saw Dan, she was positive it wasn't. She'd dreamed forever of seeing her father, but in her dreams he openly admitted who he was and pulled her into his big, comforting embrace.

"H-hello," she stuttered, willing herself to calm down. "W-we weren't expecting you."

"You would've been if you'd checked your messages," Pete pointed out with a frown.

Kay turned to the blinking red light on the desk phone. "Sorry. We've been out all day at the Polynesian Cultural Center, and we were just discussing ordering room service."

Dan stepped forward. "Don't do that. Let us take you out to dinner. We'd enjoy the company."

"Haven't you already eaten?" Shelby asked in surprise.

"No," Pete said at once. "We were waiting to talk to you two. We'd hoped to take you to lunch today, but dinner would be great compensation."

"That's a very nice invitation, Pete," Kay said with a smile, "but we've already been your guests a lot. It doesn't seem fair for you to pay for our dinner."

Dan came closer and took Kay's hand. "Let us worry about our bank accounts, Kay. I can assure you mine is quite healthy. And we'd enjoy your company."

Kay smiled at Dan before she turned to Shelby. "What do you think, Shelby? Shall we allow these gentlemen to be our escorts?"

Shelby had to hide the frown that threatened her features. Though she'd agreed to spend time with Dan and Pete in theory, actually doing it was something else again.

Pete stared at her, but it was Dan who asked the question. "Shelby, is there a problem, a reason you don't want to go to dinner with us?"

Shelby looked at Dan and then at Kay. Swallowing the emotions that roiled in her stomach like an angry sea, she replied, "I guess not. I'm just a little tired. I'm not sure I'll be good company."

Dan smiled and clapped Pete on the back. "We'll take our chances. Right, Pete?"

Chapter Ten

From the moment she'd seen Dan, Shelby had regretted her decision to go out. Now, she decided, she was being punished for her bad judgment. Every time Pete flashed her a smile or touched her hand, she felt a punch to her gut. No matter how she tried to deny it, she liked Pete.

More than liked him.

No longer did she want to play at flirting with him, kissing him. She wanted it for real. Or not at all.

But that wasn't possible.

His arm, on the back of her chair, skimmed her shoulder as he leaned forward to talk to Kay and Dan. Shelby shifted in her chair, seeking more distance between them. Pete gave her a strange look, but he continued his conversation.

When the waitress appeared with their orders, Kay told the men she was so hungry because she hadn't eaten much lunch.

"What's wrong, Kay?" Dan asked. "Did they serve poi for lunch?"

"No," she replied with a laugh. "I just didn't feel like eating. But now I'm hungry."

"I think I can afford dessert if you're a good girl and eat all your dinner," he teased.

"I've already read the dessert menu. I know just what I want."

"How about you, Shelby?" Pete asked.

When he turned that gorgeous smile on her, Shelby almost forgot his question. "No, I don't think so. I...I'm not that hungry."

"Me, neither." He touched her shoulder again and turned toward her. "What do you have planned for to-morrow?"

Whatever she planned wouldn't include him, Shelby thought. "I don't know. Maybe I'll have a lazy day on the lanai and study."

Pete stared at her. "On your lanai where no one can join you?"

"If I'm going to study, I think I'd do it best alone," she said stiffly, looking away.

"I've got a better idea," Dan interjected. "How about we go to Maui for the weekend? It's quite dif-ferent from Oahu. We can take the trip to the top of Haleakala and ride bikes back down. And we could rent a car and take the drive to Hana. Then we'd come back here Monday morning. Would you like that, Kay?"

"Oh, I'd love that. I wanted to schedule a visit to one of the other islands."

"Then it's settled," Dan said.

"I really think I should stay here and study," Shelby said, not looking at anyone.

Kay said, "Oh, Shelby, please come. Too much studying isn't good for you, you know. Besides, you've got plenty of time before the bar exam. I've heard seeing the volcano on Maui at sunrise is really special."

Shelby could read Kay's mind. She wanted to go but didn't want to be alone with Dan. Shelby looked at Dan...her dad. It hurt so much that even now he wasn't willing to claim her as his child. Then she looked at Kay. At the pleading, expectant expression on her face. How could she deny her?

"All right, Kay. I'll go." Then she slipped from her chair. "I'm really tired. I hope you'll excuse me if I go on up to bed." She didn't wait for any protests but hurried to the elevator.

Dan turned to stare after his child. How amazing this past week had been, spending time with her after so many years. "Do you think she's all right?" he asked Kay.

"Yes. I took it easy today, but Shelby was very enthusiastic. I think she volunteered every time they wanted someone to try something. And she exhibited her hula skills, too. She's getting very good at that."

"I would've liked to have seen that," Pete muttered.

Kay laughed. "Everyone in the group certainly appreciated it. In fact, one of the men attached himself to Shelby's side and she had to spend the rest of the day avoiding him."

"Damn, I should've been there with her!" Pete exclaimed.

Kay smiled even more. "While I appreciate the feeling, Pete, Shelby knows how to take care of herself. She just didn't want to hurt the man's feelings."

"Come on, Kay, you don't think she can take on a man by herself, do you?" Pete protested.

"Not only Shelby. I admit I'm not as good as she is, but I'm not totally defenseless, either," Kay said proudly. "We took the classes together."

"I didn't realize that," Dan said. "You should've told me."

"Why? You're not going to assault me, are you?"

"Of course not, sweetheart, but it relieves my mind that you can take care of yourself."

"We've been on our own for ten years now. But the reason I enrolled both of us in those classes was to give Shelby confidence in herself. Once she knew she wasn't defenseless, she recovered very quickly."

"Kay, you are an amazing woman," Dan said just as the waitress brought their desserts.

"I'm going to be a fat woman if you don't stop feeding me so well."

Dan laughed. "I'm not worried about that. It sounds like you worked it off today."

Pete looked concerned. "After all you did today, I hope Shelby will be okay for the weekend."

"It's very sweet of you to be concerned, Pete, but I'm sure she's getting some sleep already."

Before Dan could question their departure time tomorrow, Pete stood. "I'll go make the arrangements and be back in a few minutes with all the particulars," he announced.

He was gone before Kay said, "But what about your dessert?"

Dan leaned in toward her. "I think he's got his mind on something else. Shelby. Do you know what's wrong with her? She looked almost uncomfortable around us this evening."

"I think she's thinking about going back home. If she gets too involved with Pete, it's going to hurt when she leaves."

"You could be right. Of course, I'd prefer that she— and you—stay here. It's not like you have more family back in Cleveland. It makes sense to combine our family right here. You could open a store in Honolulu. I think it would make good money. And Shelby could take the bar here and practice law at my company. It would be perfect."

"It would be good for Shelby, Dan, but I'm not part of your family."

"Why not? You raised my daughter. I think that makes you part of our family. I know Shelby would agree with me."

Kay shook her head, the light in her eyes now gone.

"But I wouldn't feel right. I think I'd better go back home. There's no reason for me to stay here."

"But—"

Kay abruptly got up. "I'm going upstairs now. Call in the morning when you know when we'll leave. We'll try to be ready. Thank you for dinner." Then she fled for the elevators.

Dan sat there, frowning. He'd never met such a stubborn woman. What was it going to take to convince Kay?

"What did you do to Kay?" Pete asked as he returned to the table.

"Nothing. We were talking about why Shelby was acting so uncomfortable. Kay said it was because she was realizing leaving would be difficult if things continue to be so agreeable. So of course I suggested they stay."

"Kay wasn't interested?"

"No. I tried to tell her she was part of my family, but she wouldn't accept that. She said she needed to go back home."

"And where she goes, Shelby goes?" Pete asked slowly, despair in every word.

"I'm afraid so."

Pete moved next to Dan, giving him a clap on the back. "Since I was a kid, you've been giving me advice. Now, my friend, it's my turn to advise you. You need to tell Shelby the truth."

Dan nodded slowly, acknowledging the wisdom of Pete's words. "I know. I need to tell her before they leave. Otherwise, I'll never see her again."

"You may not anyway. She sure isn't friendly right now."

"I'm afraid you're right."

Kay tiptoed into the darkened room. She turned on the bathroom light, hoping it wouldn't awaken Shelby.

"It's okay. I'm not asleep. You can turn on the overhead light."

Kay did as Shelby said. With the light on, Shelby sat up in her bed.

"You don't look happy. What's wrong?"

"Nothing," Kay said, actually turning her back on Shelby.

"What did Dan do?"

That caused Kay to turn around. "Dan didn't do anything. Well, not much. He was concerned with how uncomfortable you suddenly seemed to be."

"What did you tell him?"

"I told him it was because you were realizing if you got any closer, the departure would be difficult."

"Good job, Kay! That makes sense."

"Yes, but then he tried to convince me we should stay. He said we should combine our family, the three of us."

"What did you tell him?"

"That I'm not his family," Kay said, and disappeared into the bathroom.

Shelby didn't chase after her. She'd heard the tears in Kay's voice even if she didn't see them, and allowed her the privacy she needed.

When Kay came out of the bathroom, dressed for

bed, Shelby said, "You know, the only thing I didn't expect from my father was that he was stupid."

"What are you talking about? Your father isn't dumb. He's built this big company from nothing. He's a very successful man."

"And yet he still can't figure out that you love him!"

Kay blushed. "I don't think I actually said I love him."

"Kay, you don't need to tell me." She wanted to reach out to her aunt. "Are you sure you don't want to just pack up and disappear?"

Kay squared her shoulders. "No, I want to go to Maui. After we get back, we'll decide what to do." When Shelby said nothing, she added, "Please?"

"Of course we'll go see Maui. You know I can't say no. But after that, we need to discuss what we're doing here. I feel like I'm submitting you to torture and you're not even protesting."

"No. The trip will be fun. Trust me, you won't ever forget it."

Shelby sighed. "That's what I'm afraid of."

Shelby was still doubting her decision in the early afternoon when the men met them in the lobby.

"When does our plane leave?" Shelby asked as Pete grabbed the one suitcase she and Kay shared.

Dan said, "We'll have about a half hour wait when we get to the airport."

"Is the flight long?" Kay asked.

"No. Just about thirty minutes," Dan said, taking Kay's hand in his.

"And you've flown between the islands before?" Shelby asked.

"Oh, yes. We ship to the other islands, so Pete or I regularly visit them to be sure everything's working okay."

Shelby looked at Pete. "Do you like Maui?"

"Absolutely. I go there whenever I want to get away for the weekend. What's better than more paradise?"

"I guess," Shelby said, still a little reluctant.

"Where do you go for the weekend when you live in Cleveland?"

"Cleveland isn't in the center of hell, you know. We live on the banks of Lake Erie," Shelby said indignantly.

"I didn't mean to— I was asking because I didn't know."

"Fine! Now you know." Shelby headed for Dan's car, parked in the driveway of the hotel.

She'd figured Kay would sit in the back with her. But when Dan ushered Kay in beside him, Pete took the backseat with her.

"I know a great restaurant near our hotel where we can have dinner," Dan said.

Pete added, "I've been to this hotel. It's very comfortable and it's right on the beach." He looked at Shelby. "We can go for a swim before we go to sleep. It's very relaxing."

Shelby gave him an attitude. "Do you think I'm tense?"

"It was just a suggestion, Shelby. After all, we have to be up to catch the van to Haleakala at three-thirty."

Her eyebrows shot up. "In the morning?"

"Of course. You don't watch a sunrise in the evening."

"But I can't— I mean—"

Kay laughed. "Shelby is not an early riser. It's all right, honey. You don't have to be alert at that hour. All you have to do is get on the van and then you can sleep until we get up to the rim of the volcano."

Still looking shell-shocked, Shelby acquiesced to their plans, but it was obvious she wasn't enthusiastic.

The short plane ride was uneventful.

"Does flying bother you?" Pete asked after they took off. Once again he sat beside her.

"I don't like it, but I recognize the necessity of it," Shelby grumbled.

"What do you do to entertain yourself during the flight?"

"I usually watch the movie they show." She looked up front but there was no screen.

"Sorry, the flight's too short. But you can look out the window. You might be able to see something interesting."

Shelby shuddered. "No, I don't like to look out the window, especially over water."

Pete chuckled. "I guess that's why you insisted I take the window seat."

"Yes, it is." Shelby stared straight ahead.

"Well, you could tell me your life story. Or I could tell you mine."

"No, thank you. I prefer to close my eyes and just

wait until the flight is over." In truth, Shelby would've liked to hear Pete's life story. She didn't know that much about him, but she figured he'd be easier to forget, the less she knew.

Luckily, he took the hint and didn't bother her anymore. Only a few minutes later, they began their descent.

The hotel was every bit as nice as Pete had said. As they pulled up, a pathway afforded them a view of the beautiful beach. Shelby wanted to suggest they swim before dinner, but she didn't think Kay would agree. So she merely followed her up to their room, which had an even larger lanai than their room in Honolulu.

"Oh, this is very nice," Kay exclaimed as they came in.

"Yes, it is nice, but it's still just a hotel room. I think I'm getting ready to go home."

"It does wear on you, doesn't it?" Kay agreed.

"Yes, it does. If I had a home like Dan, I don't think I'd ever want to go away."

"I think he offered this trip as a way to keep you close to him, honey."

"I think you're the one he's staying close to, Kay."

Kay grabbed Shelby's arm as she turned away. "Honey, you're not jealous of me, are you?"

"No, of course not. And if he offered to make you happy, I'd be delighted. But he's not doing that, nor is he claiming me as his daughter. All he's doing is making a mess of everything."

"Do you wish I hadn't insisted on the trip?" Kay asked.

Shelby shook her head. "Don't mind me, Kay. I'm just

being crabby. I'll try to cheer up before dinner. I promise."

"Well, you don't have long, honey. We've got to meet the guys in twenty minutes."

"I think I'll go out on the lanai and look at the ocean for a few minutes. That'll remind me why we're here—to see the sights of Maui." With a smile she slipped outside and stretched out on the chaise lounge.

The solitude and the peaceful surroundings helped Shelby gain control of her emotions. She decided to try to delude herself that she knew nothing about Dan. Or Pete. The last was harder to do. It was tempting to remember his touch, his kisses, his warmth. Maybe the weekend would be bearable if she treated him as a stranger. A stranger who only wanted to get close to the boss's daughter.

Except she'd decided to forget that she was the boss's daughter. After all, she might as well. Her father certainly had.

"Shelby? It's only a couple of minutes before we need to go down," Kay called softly from the sliding door.

Shelby swung her legs off the lounge and stood. "Fine. I'll just rebraid my hair," she said, smiling at Kay.

She let out a sigh of relief. "I'm so glad that helped, honey."

"Happiness is a state of mind, Kay. You helped me learn that. I'm going to be happy until we get back to Honolulu."

"Thank you, honey." Kay hugged Shelby tightly. A

few minutes later they took the elevator to the lobby to meet their escorts.

"Here they are." Dan gave them a big smile as they exited the elevator. "The restaurant is just across the street." He reached out for Kay's hand and led her away.

Pete stood there, just watching Shelby.

"Aren't we going with them?" she asked, suddenly edgy.

"I would assume so. Shall I stay about six feet from you, or do you want to take my hand?"

"I think two feet would be sufficient. After all, I don't consider you dangerous."

"I don't know whether I should say thank you or be insulted," Pete said with a rueful look. Then he swept his hand forward and bowed slightly. "Shall we go?"

"Yes, thank you." She didn't think he knew what she was thanking him for, which was a good thing. But she was grateful for the distance. She could handle the evening as long as he stayed two feet away.

Chapter Eleven

She made it all the way to after-dinner drinks.

While the rest of the foursome went to the penthouse club, Shelby went up to her room. Once there, she was much too restless to go to sleep. She suddenly remembered Pete mentioning a late swim. That was exactly what she needed. Stepping onto the lanai, she saw the beach was illuminated by several lights.

With a smile, she returned to the room and donned her one-piece suit and cover-up and headed back to the elevator bare-footed.

The water was silky smooth and warm still from the hot sun. She waded in, gradually going a little deeper, enjoying the feel of it against her skin.

"Happier now?"

Shelby jerked around only to find Pete in the water beside her. "Wh-what are you doing here?"

"Same as you. I wasn't ready for bed, and a little tension had built up for some reason." He paused and then added, "I decided to come for a swim."

"Oh. M-me, too."

"Look, Shelby, I don't know what went wrong. If you don't want to tell me, that's your business. Why don't we pretend we just met tonight and enjoy the swim? It's lonely swimming alone."

"I...I'd like that."

"Okay. Hi. I'm Pete. You a stranger to Maui?"

"Yes, I am. I'm Shelby."

"Well, welcome to Hawaii, Shelby. I'm an old hand since I live in Hawaii. Let me show you the beach."

"What is there to show about a beach? There's sand, water, a few shells."

"But what about under the water?"

"I don't think I swim well enough to go underwater."

"Too bad. I know some great places to scuba dive."

"Maybe the next time I visit."

"You're sure you're going home?"

Shelby held herself still. "Yes, I'm sure," she said firmly, not looking at him.

"I see. Then we'd best enjoy tonight." He splashed her, taunting her to retaliate. On reflex, she splashed him and they began a game of tag that consumed a lot of energy and left them exhausted and stretched out on the sand half an hour later.

Shelby rolled over onto her stomach. "That was fun, and it released a lot of that tension, too."

"Maybe it'll help you get to sleep."

"It's not that late. Are you going to bed this early?"

"Have you forgotten that we're leaving at 3:30 a.m.?"

"Oh. Are we back to knowing each other?"

"We can only pretend for so long, Shelby."

"I guess so." She started to get up, but Pete caught hold of her arm.

"Wait. Will you please tell me what I've done that was so terrible?"

The warmth of his hand on her wrist brought back all the feelings she'd experienced when he'd touched her before. She didn't want to pull away but she had to. "I can't."

"Why not?"

"The time has passed, Pete. I can't forget that I'm going home soon." Using Kay's excuse that she'd given Dan seemed like a good idea to Shelby.

"So you're not interested in making more memories?"

"Yes, I am, but I think I need to limit the memories to those I can see." She meant the sights on Maui. But Pete interpreted her words differently.

"Well, here I am, right in front of you."

He'd taken her by surprise. "I don't mean— You know what I meant, Pete. I want to remember the beaches, the mountains, the ocean."

"But not me?"

Shelby blinked rapidly, praying she wouldn't cry in front of Pete. "Of course I'll remember you. You were very kind to me."

"Kind?" he demanded in a low growl. "That's not how I want you to remember me." He leaned over, pulled her toward him and kissed her.

For one brief moment, Shelby was overcome by longing, by the feel of his warm body pressed against her. She'd pretended she hadn't been moved by Pete's caresses, but she'd lied. To herself and to Pete. But she couldn't tell him now.

She just pulled away and shook her head. "I have to go up now."

He let her go, but his gaze remained fixed on her as she again entered the ocean to wash the sand off her body. When she came out, she put on her cover-up and headed for the hotel without a word to him.

"Shelby? It's time to get up. You've got about ten minutes to throw on some clothes. Hurry, we don't want to miss the van."

"But it's dark outside," Shelby said, and turned over to hide her eyes from the light.

Kay turned back the cover and pulled Shelby to a sitting position. "I've already finished in the bathroom. Get in there now. And hurry."

Shelby staggered to the bathroom. If it weren't for the bright light, she might've managed to fall asleep in there, but Kay kept prompting her through the door. When she came out, Kay thrust some clothes at her.

"Put these on. It's time to go."

"What are these?"

"Dan remembered last night that it's cold up on the volcano. You'll need these to keep warm."

Shelby discovered what she held was a sweatshirt and warm-up pants. "You're kidding?"

"No. Put them on so we can go. And don't forget your sunglasses. It's going to be bright when you get on the bike."

Somehow, Shelby didn't quite process those words. But she managed to slip into the sweats, though they felt too warm to be comfortable. When she started pulling them off, Kay stopped her by opening the door and shoving her through it.

"To the elevators," Kay insisted, and Shelby stumbled along beside her.

When they reached the brightly lit lobby, Dan and Pete were waiting for them. Once they were seated in the van, Pete was quite surprised when Shelby curled up against him and began breathing deeply.

"Kay, is she all right?" he whispered.

Kay looked over her shoulder and smiled. "Yes. She just doesn't wake up this early in the morning. If she's bothering you, I can sit next to her."

"I've got no problem with her sleeping on me, as long as you don't mention it to her when she wakes up."

"Deal," Dan said for both him and Kay.

Pete settled back against the seat, his arm wrapped around Shelby, cuddling her close.

* * *

"Okay, here comes the sun!" a loud voice announced, disturbing Shelby's comfort. She twisted a little and moaned, sniffing something elusive yet familiar. What was it? She sifted through the information stored in her brain and finally identified the scent.

"Mmm, Pete," she said softly. That was it. That was Pete's scent he always wore. She loved it.

"Yeah, honey, I'm here," Pete whispered.

Suddenly Shelby jerked upright, her eyes wide open. "What are you doing?"

"Waiting for the sunrise. What are you doing?"

"I…I was sleeping!"

"I know. On my shoulder."

"No!" Shelby protested.

"Here comes the sun!" someone announced again.

"Why do they keep saying that?" Shelby demanded.

"Because we all came up here to see the sunrise, honey," Kay said softly. "Don't you remember?"

"Oh, yeah," Shelby said in a shamed whisper. She straightened her spine and stared straight ahead, but she found it difficult to take in the scene. They were seated on benches on a landscape that made her think of the moon as she'd seen it on TV.

Suddenly it started drizzling, and clouds rolled above them. She looked at Pete, wondering what they were going to do now.

"I think it's only going to last a few minutes if you want to wait in the van," one of the guides announced.

Dan looked at Kay and Shelby. "I don't think it will last long, like he said. Do you mind a little rain?"

Shelby was suddenly aware of a chill in the air and the sweatsuit she was wearing. "Where did this come from?"

"Dan bought them for us last night because he'd forgotten to tell us to bring something warm," Kay said. "Wasn't that nice of him?"

"Yes, uh, thanks, Dan."

"It was my pleasure, and you look quite fetching in yours," he added with a grin.

Shelby couldn't smile back. She hadn't had time to work up her resolve to enjoy the weekend. Instead, this morning, it seemed much too difficult to smile at her father when he'd never acknowledged her, or to appreciate Pete's closeness when she knew he only wanted to gain favor with his boss.

"I think I'll wait in the van," she said abruptly and got up from the bench.

But just as she reached the van, the guide announced the rain had halted. He invited everyone back to the bench seats. Shelby found herself turned around by the crowd and forced back to the benches.

"Come on, it's all right," Pete whispered in her ear.

She jerked away in surprise. "I'm sorry. It's too early…"

"It's all right. I know you're trying to work something out. I'll give you some space, okay?"

"Please," she said with a big sigh.

He took her hand and led her back to the place they had earlier occupied. Dan gave her a close look, but he nodded to Pete. She guessed Pete had gained some Brownie points by coming after her, but she didn't care. He'd made the situation easier.

As if on cue, the clouds broke apart and the sun rose in the eastern sky. The brilliant redness of the orb made it easy to believe it was a mass of flames, rather than a distant body in the sky.

In only minutes the red had faded to orange and everyone began standing and stretching.

"What are they doing now?" she whispered to Pete.

He stared at her. "You really don't remember anything, do you?"

"What am I supposed to remember?"

"We're riding bikes down to sea level."

"I don't have a— Oh! You said last night we would ride bikes but I didn't bring one. How can I—"

"They provide the bikes. All you have to do is ride." He pulled her up from the bench. "Come on. We'll go stretch a little."

When they were all four on bicycles going down the mountain, following the leader, who seemed able to ride his bicycle almost backward, Shelby wanted to remove the sweatsuit.

It didn't seem that they intended to stop, however, so she managed to push up her sleeves and let the breeze cool her.

After the exhilarating ride down, the van took them back to their hotel. Shelby could scarcely keep her eyes open for lunch. Then she went up to the room for a long nap.

* * *

"What's wrong with Shelby?" Dan asked Kay.

"It's like I told you. She's worried about leaving. She said last night that she was a little weary of being in a hotel. I know what she means."

"You, too, huh? Are you worried about leaving?"

"It's never easy to return to reality after time in paradise."

"But I think you could bring your business here and do well. I could bankroll you for a few months until you started showing a profit. It would be—"

"Impossible. I'm sorry, Dan. I know you mean well, but I think you've ridden that idea to death."

"What if I talk Shelby into staying? Would you stay then?"

"No, I can't." She suddenly pushed her chair back from the table. "I believe I'll take a nap, too."

"We'll see you later for dinner. I'll call about the time," Dan called after her.

As Kay left the restaurant, Pete came back in, having escorted Shelby to the elevator. He sat down across from Dan.

"Looks like you did about as well as I did."

Dan nodded. "Kay won't stay."

"Neither will Shelby."

"There's got to be something neither one of us is getting. But I guess we'll have to wait for them to tell us." Dan tried to pump up himself and his friend with a little optimism. "We've still got a little more than twenty-four hours before we land back in Honolulu."

It didn't work on Pete. "Yeah. I hope that's enough time."

* * *

The next day, after a leisurely breakfast, they all got in a rented car to drive to Hana, a small town on the other side of the island. Several wealthy families had lived there, including Charles Lindbergh, and the drive was supposed to have spectacular views of waterfalls and the coastline.

Pete was the driver, much to Shelby's relief. She could enjoy his company without any chance of him touching her. During the first few miles Shelby couldn't believe the beauty of the waterfalls and coastline. She was exclaiming so much, she didn't notice the quiet in the backseat until she turned around to make sure Kay saw the next waterfall.

After one look at her aunt, Shelby almost climbed over the back of her seat to reach her. "Kay, what's wrong?"

Kay didn't speak. She shook her head and pressed her hand to her lips.

"Pete, can you pull over?" Shelby asked. "I think Kay is carsick." She looked at Dan sitting beside Kay. "Why didn't you say something?"

"I didn't know. I thought she was still upset about… things, so I didn't press her."

Pete found a narrow place to pull over. There wasn't a lot of room, but Shelby got out and opened the door for Kay. "Get out, honey, and breathe deeply."

After a couple of minutes Kay shook her head. "I'm so sorry, Shelby, but I can't go any farther. If Pete can't turn the car around, I'll just wait beside the road until you come back this way."

That told Shelby how awful Kay was feeling. She put her head in the car to speak to Pete. "Can you turn the car around?"

"Sure, if Dan will get out and hold up traffic," he agreed.

"I'll do it. But first I'm going to put Kay in the front seat and open the window. Hopefully she won't get as sick up here."

Shelby marched around the next curve and stood in the middle of the one-lane road, holding out a hand to stop the cars. Dan did the same in the other direction, while Pete completed the turn. Then they jumped in the backseat.

Kay thanked them. "It's better up here, but I still don't feel like going on. I'm so sorry to ruin the day for the rest of you."

"Don't be silly, my girl," Dan assured her. "We've been to Hana. We were only going for you two."

Shelby reached forward to pat Kay on the shoulder. "Just lie back and relax. We'll be back at the hotel in no time."

In actual fact, it took them about an hour to reach the hotel. Dan insisted on helping Kay to the elevator, and Shelby waited to thank Pete for acting quickly and being agreeable about the change.

Pete didn't exhibit the reaction she expected. Nearly exploding, he shouted, "Did you really think I would insist on going on with Kay so sick? Do you think I'm that insensitive, Shelby? Is that what's wrong? I don't seem sensitive enough?"

"No! No, that's not what's wrong. I just wanted to thank you for making the change so easy. That's all." She turned away for the elevators.

Pete grabbed her arm, holding her back, suddenly contrite. "Honey, wait! Can't we at least talk a little? I feel like I've lost something very dear to me."

"Don't!" she protested, pulling away as her eyes filled with tears. "I...I have to go see about Kay."

"How's Kay?" Pete asked when Dan reached their room.

"I don't know. She didn't want me to even help her to her room. Something's gone very wrong and I don't know what to do. Do you?"

Pete was hardly the person to ask, not after the mess he'd just made. "Not me. I made Shelby cry just by asking what was wrong."

"Damn! What's the matter with those two? I just don't understand them. Maybe we can discuss things at dinner."

"What's there to discuss, Dan? We love them and they don't love us."

"Do you?"

"Do I what?"

"Love my daughter?"

Pete didn't have to stop to think. "Yeah. I can't seem to think of much else. And the thought of her leaving has me wanting to buy a one-way ticket to Cleveland. Can you imagine me, an island boy, wanting to go live on the mainland?"

Dan gave a shaky laugh. "Do you mind company on that trip to Cleveland?"

"No, but who'd run the company with both of us gone?"

"We'll find someone. Right now we have the rest of the week to work on them before we have to buy those tickets."

The phone ringing woke both women from their naps. Shelby got up to answer the phone, but Kay must've realized who it was, because she sat up and shook her head. Then she rushed into the bathroom to be sick.

"Um, Dan, I don't think Kay's going to be able to go to dinner. She's still not feeling well."

"Should we get the hotel doctor to check on her?" Shelby heard the concern in his voice.

She relayed his question to Kay as she came out of the bathroom and crawled back into bed. Kay shook her head.

"Dan, she'll be all right in the morning," Shelby told him.

After hanging up the phone, she sat down beside Kay on her bed. "Feel any better?"

"A little."

"So do you want to go have dinner with Dan and Pete?"

"No. Do you?"

Shelby shook her head. "I've lost my ability to pretend, I'm afraid."

"Me, too. Something reminded Dan about your mother, and he made several comments in the car on the way to Hana. It only confirmed what I'd believed all along. There is no way he'd ever marry into our family again."

"Oh, Kay, I'm so sorry." Shelby wrapped her arms around her aunt. "Are you sorry we ever came?"

"No, I'm not. I wanted you to know that your mother's opinion of your father was wrong. That he's a good man, and you'll find a good man one day, too, if you'll just let yourself."

"Oh, Kay," Shelby said, tears running down her cheeks. "You made such a sacrifice for me."

"Not too much of a sacrifice," Kay said with a smile through her tears. "I got to pretend for a little while."

"So what now? Do we go home after we get back to Honolulu?" Shelby asked.

"That's what I want to do, but don't you want to stay until your father says something to you?"

"And how many years do you think that would take? After all, I'm twenty-four!"

"Oh, honey, you can't blame him. He thinks you'll probably hate him. Of course he's not eager to tell you."

"Then I see no point in staying."

"Well, if you're sure," Kay said quietly, "then I guess we're going home."

Chapter Twelve

On the flight back to Oahu the two women sat together, unwilling to let either man get close. They said all the right things, but they still clung to each other.

When they reached the Honolulu hotel, Kay shook Dan's hand. "Thank you for your hospitality and generosity, Dan."

"Kay, you know I've enjoyed it more than you. How about dinner this evening to make up for last night?"

"Why don't we talk later and see?"

Dan frowned. "Kay, is something wrong?"

"No, of course not. I'm just still recovering from yesterday."

He bent forward and kissed her temple. "Okay, get some rest. I'll call you in a couple of hours."

Pete and Shelby had stood there listening to their

goodbyes. When Pete turned to her, she said, "You've both been very generous." And then she slipped into the elevator with Kay and punched the button for their floor.

"That sounded remarkably like a kiss-off," Pete said slowly.

Dan jerked around to stare at his friend. "What do you mean? Kay still doesn't feel well. You can understand that. And Shelby's been unhappy the entire weekend. She'll come around in a day or two."

Pete just shook his head.

Shelby found Kay stretched across her bed, sobbing. Shelby had gone into the bathroom for a few minutes. In only that short space of time, Kay had lost control.

Shelby stood there, wanting to comfort her aunt. Instead, she whirled around and ran out of the room. She couldn't comfort Kay, but she could give her a chance at happiness, if her father would cooperate.

She stepped out of the elevator and saw Dan talking to someone at the hotel desk. She moved to within his line of vision, and he abruptly ended the conversation and hurried to her side. "Shelby, is Kay all right?"

"Yes, she is. The problem is with you."

"What are you talking about?"

"I'm talking about you being a stupid man," Shelby told him, trying to hold back her anger but failing.

"What— How—"

"Kay is upstairs crying because we're leaving today.

She loves you. If you have any feelings for her, you'll get in the elevator and go tell her!"

The emotions that chased across Dan's face relieved Shelby. She'd been afraid she'd misread his intentions. He suddenly wrapped her in a tight embrace and kissed her temple. "Thank you, Shelby. I'll talk to you later. Right now I'm going to Kay."

"Yes," she agreed. Then she found a seat to sit and wait for whatever happened a few floors up.

"Why are you crying?"

She gasped and looked up to see Pete standing beside her. She hastily wiped her tears away, tears she hadn't even known were sliding down her cheeks. "I'm...I'm not crying!"

He reached out and caught a stray tear on his finger. "Then what's this?"

"Nothing."

"Have you seen Dan?"

Shelby nodded but said nothing.

"Did he make you cry?"

She shook her head.

Pete sat in the chair next to her and caught her hand in his. "Then why are you crying?"

She closed her eyes and pulled her hand from his. "I can't talk to you."

"Why not?"

"You wouldn't understand."

"So you've said. If you can't explain, can you at least tell me why you're sitting here?"

"I have to give Dan and Kay some privacy."

"Okay. I have to wait for him. May I wait with you?"

"Yes, as long as you don't talk to me."

He sat beside her, helplessly watching the tears that continued to escape her eyes, unable to do anything to help her. The only thing he could imagine was Kay saying goodbye to Dan.

Which meant Shelby would be leaving as well.

Suddenly Pete felt like crying, too.

Kay thought Shelby had forgotten her key when she heard someone knocking on the door. She didn't know where Shelby had gone, but she'd probably decided to get a drink.

Kay rolled off the bed and hastily wiped her cheeks. "I'm coming," she called out. When she swung open the door, she almost passed out. There was Dan. Handsome, wonderful Dan.

"Did you forget something?"

"Yeah," he said, staring at her face. "I forgot this." He pulled her into his arms and kissed her, and wondered why he hadn't done that long before now.

When he finally released her, he moved into the room with his arm around Kay's small waist. "Shelby—my wonderful daughter—said you have feelings for me. I'm hoping that's true. It feels like it's true."

"Shelby shouldn't have— I don't think—"

"Because I came to say I have feelings for you. Very strong feelings that began with the respect I felt for a teenager trying to save a grown man and a little girl."

"I just wanted to help."

"And you did. Then you rescued the child and took her into your home and raised her as if she was your own."

"Dan, don't make me a hero. Shelby is a terrific child. I mean woman."

"I know she is, sweetheart. I'm trying to explain how my feelings developed. You began writing more often and sending pictures. You shared my daughter with me every step of the way. That was a wonderful gift."

"I wanted you to know she was loved and cared for."

"I knew it from your letters. But I also got to know you. Not the teenager, but the woman you've become. When I saw you here the first night, it all crystallized in me. I knew then that I didn't want you to leave. Now I'm so scared you will that I can hardly think."

"Oh, Dan!" Kay sighed, reaching up to cup his face.

He covered her hand. "Tell me you have feelings for me, please? I'll give you time, but don't go away."

Kay, finally believing what he'd been saying, let her arms encircle his neck and leaned forward to whisper, "Who's asking for time?"

Dan's face lit up with love and he wrapped her in his arms, promising in his heart to never let her go.

It was almost an hour before Dan and Kay returned to earth long enough to think about Shelby. They hurried down to the lobby to find Shelby and Pete sitting silently beside each other.

"I'm sorry we took so long, Shelby," Dan said, suddenly feeling awkward.

"If you made Kay happy, you're forgiven," she said, a smile on her face, but it didn't appear genuine to Dan.

Kay spoke before he could. "I am happy, honey. Thank you so much. Dan wants us to go to his house for lunch. Is that okay? We have a lot to discuss."

"I imagine you do, but I bet you can do it better without an audience. I'll see you later." Shelby stood, not meeting any of their gazes, and ran for the elevator, leaving the trio in shock.

Dan looked at Kay in confusion. "What's she talking about? Of course we need her to make plans."

Pete stepped forward. "Shelby has been sitting down here suffering, crying. She wouldn't talk about anything. My guess is she's upstairs packing."

"Pete's right. I've got to go to her." Kay started to bolt, the sudden movement spurring Dan to action. He grabbed her arm to hold her in place.

"No," he said firmly. "I've got to." Then he turned to Pete. "Call Betty, please, and tell her we'll be there in an hour to have a celebratory lunch for four."

Without another word he set out to do what should've been done a long time ago.

When he reached the hotel room, his hand was nearly shaking as he rapped on the door. The moment he'd waited for had finally come, but when he looked at his daughter, he suddenly forgot all the words he'd practiced.

Behind her he saw Pete was right. Shelby was packing her bag.

"Honey, you can't go," he said at once.

"Why can't I?" she asked without looking at him.

"Because I need to talk to you. To explain to you why I didn't say anything...about being your father." There, the word was out.

But Shelby still didn't look at him.

"It's all right," she said. "I understand."

"You do?" He wanted to reach out to her so badly. To lift her face up to his so she could see the pain in his eyes. "You understand how afraid I was that you'd run as fast as you could in the opposite direction if you knew who I really was?"

"I...I wouldn't have done that."

"No? I know your mother said terrible things about me. Why wouldn't you believe her? After all, she was there and I wasn't."

Shelby sank onto her bed. "I'd begun to realize how crazy she was. I guessed she was part of the reason you left."

"Part?" he asked. "What other reason would I have?"

"Me. I figured you weren't ready for a child. A lot of men aren't."

"Oh, baby, I didn't leave because I didn't want to be a father. I wanted that more than anything. The first time I held you in my arms, it...it was as if the world had begun anew. I immediately had visions of your first word, your first step, your first kiss.... I wanted to be there for every first you ever had."

"You did?" Shelby asked in wonder, finally looking up at him. He could see the tears glistening in her eyes.

"Oh, yes. I did. My best times were when your mother would go out and it would just be you, me and Kay. We had great times then, but I guess you don't remember them."

"I…I remember my first trip to the zoo. I think you must've been there, too, but when we got home, Mom was there and…she started screaming. I remember Kay taking me to my room and holding me while Mom shrieked in the other room. I kept listening for something—I think it was your voice—but I never heard it."

"No, you didn't," Dan said slowly. "That was the last time I saw you. Kay called me that night and begged me to go away, to save you from any more attacks from Cordy. She hated me because I left her. And she was using you to punish me. All I could do was agree with Kay. I didn't want your mother to hurt you. When she lost her temper, no one knew what she'd do."

Shelby nodded, the tears streaming down her cheeks now.

"I'm so sorry, baby," Dan said, kneeling down and wrapping his arms around his daughter. How he'd yearned, for so many years, to do just this. "I'm sorry if I made the wrong decision, Shelby. I didn't know what to do but to go away. But I always wanted you. I have a shrine to you in my bedroom at home. Every picture Kay sent me. I almost threw my arms around you when I first saw you, but you stuck out your hand to remind me we were strangers."

Shelby put her arms around his neck and hugged him. "I'm glad you didn't forget me."

"Never. I called Kay to ask if I could come see you or you could come see me after she took you in, but she pleaded with me to leave you there."

"She told me. She wanted Mom to stay nearby. If you'd shown up then, it would've sent her over the edge. Now, looking back, I believe Kay was right. But I wish I'd known that you…you hadn't forgotten me."

"I'm sorry for that, baby. But you know now." Dan took her hand and stood. "Finish packing your bag. I'm going to send Kay up to pack, too. Both of you are coming to my house. We'll have lunch and talk about plans. Will you come home with me?"

"Yes, I will."

He kissed her cheek. "Thank you, Shelby, thank you so much."

Then he strode out the door, his shoulders a little straighter, his walk a little more confident.

"What do you mean you're not staying?" Dan roared, staring at Shelby.

The four of them were having lunch at his house after their emotional morning.

"I'm returning to Cleveland." Shelby kept her gaze on her lunch, avoiding everyone's eyes.

"But, Shelby, you said you forgave me! Why won't you stay?"

"I can't. I'm sorry, but I just can't."

Kay, sitting beside Dan, touched his hand. He turned to her, then he asked, "But what about the wedding? You've got to be here for the wedding."

"You've got five days, Dan. Can you get married by Friday?"

"I guess, but I don't understand."

Shelby smiled briefly at her father. "Then I'll be here for the wedding."

Dan turned to Kay. "Can't you talk to her?"

"I'll try, but she's your daughter, Dan. You know how stubborn *you* get."

"If he doesn't, I do," Pete muttered.

Kay bent over to kiss Dan before she stood. "If you gentlemen will excuse us, Shelby and I need to get together with Betty and start making lists. Otherwise we won't manage to have a wedding by Friday." She picked up the dishes around her to take to the kitchen. Shelby did the same and followed her aunt out of the room.

"Have you managed to talk to her yet?" Dan asked Pete when they were alone.

"No. She's avoided me at every turn. I don't think it will do me any good to talk to her. She's crossed me off her list."

"I think you're the reason she's leaving. I really want her to stay."

"Then I'll go away, Dan. I owe you that, at least."

"No, son, you don't owe me anything. And I couldn't manage without you. We're partners and we'll stay partners."

Dan's house was a stir of activity. Betty was showing the caterers where to set up; Kay was directing the florist where to place the flowers. When Pete arrived, he greeted both of those ladies with a smile, then cocked an eyebrow, forming a question that Kay answered with a nod toward the lanai.

He stepped outside and spotted the object of his search. Shelby was stretched out on the lounge on the lanai, absorbing some rays. When Pete cast a shadow over her, she opened her eyes and saw him.

"Taking it easy?" he asked. "Everyone in the house is scurrying around. I thought you would be, too. The wedding is only four hours away."

"And what would you have me do? Shoo Betty from her kitchen, where she reigns supreme? Or should I take away Kay's pleasure of arranging her own wedding?"

"You think neither of them wants your assistance?"

"I know they don't."

"Are you still going home tomorrow?" Pete asked abruptly. After all, in the past few days he hadn't been able to find time alone with Shelby to ask that important question.

"Yes." She didn't bother to look at him.

"If I asked you to marry me, would you stay?"

"No."

"That's it? Just a casual no when I ask you to marry me?"

"What do you want me to say? No, thank you?"

Pete sat down beside her on the lounge. "Something's been bugging you since you found out Dan was your father. That was what changed things, wasn't it?"

Shelby looked away.

"There's no reason not to tell me now. We're practically going to be family."

"You wish!" Shelby snapped.

"Damn it, Shelby, come clean. I need to know what I did."

"Like you don't know. You made a play for the boss's daughter to improve your career!"

Pete stared at her, shocked. Finally he leaned forward. "You believed that? No wonder you wouldn't talk to me! But I think it would be hard to understand, since I own forty percent of his company." He stood. "I didn't need you to get in good with Dan. I was already there."

"How could you own forty percent of the company? You can't be older than thirty."

"Twenty-nine, to be exact."

"Well, then, explain!"

"I told you Dan was my Big Brother when I was a teenager. He helped me figure out what I wanted to do with my life and gave me a scholarship to the university if I'd come to work for him for the first four years after I got out. That was no hardship since he's got a very good company. He taught me about saving and investing. Then he offered to let me buy in last year."

"So why did you fall in with Dan's plan?"

"What plan? Did you ever find out what it is?"

"No. But I guess we could ask Dan now."

"I guess we could." He walked to the door. "Kay, where is Dan?"

"He's in his bedroom, packing for our honeymoon,"

she announced, enthusiasm in her voice. Pete couldn't hold back a smile. She was too infectious.

"Wait here," he called over his shoulder.

About two minutes later he returned with Dan beside him.

"Did you tell him what to say?" Shelby demanded.

"To say about what?" Dan asked, his brow furrowed.

"How do I know you'll tell me the truth?" Shelby asked her father.

"Shelby, I've done many wrong things as your father, but I've never lied to you, and I never will. What do you want to know?"

"I heard you speak of a plan concerning Kay and myself. I want to know what the plan was and how much you told Pete."

"I wanted to have time to get to know you, and I wanted to spend time with Kay. I thought that would be more easily accomplished if I had a second gentle-man to make a foursome. I asked Pete to come along."

"And you explained that to Pete?"

"Sure. He did it as a favor to me."

"And?" Shelby persisted.

"And I wouldn't have objected if you and Pete con-nected, formed an attachment. It would've meant you stayed and I thought it would mean Kay would stay… without me having to make a fool of myself first," Dan said with a rueful smile. "Fortunately, you took pity on me and told me about Kay's feelings. I hope you know how much I appreciate it, Shelby. And how much I wish you'd stay here."

"Thanks, Dan. When did you let Pete know what you wanted?"

"He guessed the general direction of my plans. And I'll admit he didn't object, either. After all, he'd spent some time with you."

Shelby said, "Thank you, but—"

Pete interrupted whatever she was going to say. "If you'll excuse us, Dan, Shelby and I have some issues to discuss. We'll see you at the wedding."

"Oh, uh, yes, I'm counting on it."

Pete remained silent, as did Shelby, until Dan had entered the house and closed the door.

"Now do you believe me?"

"I…I suppose you're right. It doesn't sound like either of you had any idea about what you were going to do."

"Then what's your excuse for rejecting my proposal now?"

"Did it ever occur to you that maybe I don't love you?" she asked defensively.

"Nope. Not after we kissed on the beach. Shelby, you mean too much to me to let you wander away. At least stay awhile and let's explore what's happening between us."

"I…I have to prepare for the bar exam!"

"Make it the Hawaii bar and I'm all in agreement." He sat back down beside her. "What are you rushing home for? You got some guy waiting for your return?"

"No!"

"Look, I'm not insisting you marry me at once, like Dan did Kay, but I don't want you to go. You can stay here in the house while they're on their honeymoon. I can visit, we can have dinner here with Betty doing the cooking."

"So you're too cheap to take me out?"

He relaxed as he caught the teasing glint in her eyes and pulled her into his arms for one of those kisses he had earlier mentioned. It was so good, he took several more. Then he released her, muttering in her ear, "You're going to drive me crazy, young lady!"

"Then you'll have company. I almost lost my mind these past few days."

"Damn, now we've got to wait until they return from their honeymoon, and they're taking two weeks!"

"So you're not going to rush me, huh?"

He smiled. "That was before I kissed you again. Which I should've done sooner, you know. You can tell a lot by how a woman kisses."

"Oh, really? How many women have you kissed?"

Pete seemed to realize he'd made a mistake. "Maybe we should go ask Kay and Dan if they can come back in a week for our wedding."

"Why spoil their honeymoon?"

"Because I think it's going to be hard to wait for mine if we spend much time together."

Shelby, feeling more confident now, leaned forward for another kiss. "You know, you still haven't told me you love me."

Pete cupped her face and looked deep into the blue eyes he'd never tire of. "I do, Shelby. I love you."

"And I love you, Pete." She kissed him again, giving him a taste of paradise.

Epilogue

Once again two women were scurrying around Dan's house, preparing for a wedding. Only this time it was Shelby's.

"All right, child, it's time for you to start getting ready. Go on, I'll do that," Betty ordered as Shelby tweaked one of the floral arrangements.

With a grin, Shelby hugged Betty and kissed her cheek. "Yes, ma'am. Has Dan and Kay's plane landed yet?"

"It should've hit the tarmac about thirty minutes ago. They'll be getting here any minute, and so will your groom. So hurry now. He's not supposed to see you on your wedding day."

"I know. Thanks, Betty, for all the work you've done for me and for taking care of Pete and me this week."

"It's been my pleasure. I always did think this house was too quiet."

"You may hear the patter of little feet soon since Kay wants to have children right away."

"I think that's a good decision. Your daddy is a good man. He needs to experience all the trials and tribulations of raising a child. He'll appreciate his wife more."

"I couldn't agree more," Shelby said with a big smile.

When they both heard a car door closing, Shelby let out a little scream and headed for her bedroom. "Send Kay in to see me right away!" she called over her shoulder.

Betty turned to the front door, opening it before they could even knock. She gave Kay a big hug, then Dan and Pete, too. After bringing them into the house, she sent Kay to Shelby's room and Dan and Pete to the master bedroom for the moment.

"Betty's as bossy as ever, I see," Dan said with a smile.

"Yeah, but she was great this week. She spoiled us rotten, of course. And now that I'm getting married, I've been informed by my future wife that I need a house like yours and a housekeeper like Betty!"

"Good. Glad to hear you'll be treating my little girl right."

"Yeah, and I hope we pay her a big salary so I can afford to treat her right." Shelby had agreed to join Island Traders as legal counsel once she passed the Hawaii bar exam. Pete's grin told Dan he wasn't really worried.

"So how was the honeymoon?" he asked.

"Much better than my first one. But then, going to a drive-in movie would've been better than that fiasco. We had a wonderful time."

"What did you show her on the Big Island?"

Dan's face turned beet-red and he avoided Pete's surprised look. "Oh, just about everything."

"Didn't leave the hotel room, did you?" Pete teased.

"No, and you probably won't, either, you randy teenager!"

"Hey, I'm twenty-nine," Pete protested.

"Yeah, and I'm forty-six, and she still makes me feel like a awkward eighteen-year-old sometimes."

"Good. I can't wait for my turn."

"Then get in the shower so you can dress in that monkey suit of yours!"

Shelby eased the wedding dress over her head and slid it down her body. The white satin skirt, gored from the hips, settled down around her. The formfitting bodice, studded with pearls, flattered her nicely tanned arms and shoulders.

"Oh, honey, you look wonderful!" Kay exclaimed.

"I hoped you'd like it. Betty and I looked at everything they had in stock. But we both liked this one best."

"I can't believe I missed preparing for your wedding."

"Well, you were kind of busy. But you took time off to come back for our wedding. We appreciate that, Kay."

"I was anxious to get home anyway. You know how hotels are."

"Yes," Shelby said with a laugh.

"Okay, it's time for the veil. Can you kneel on the bed? I want to be sure I get it centered." Kay put the veil on her niece and backed away, tears in her eyes. "You are the most beautiful bride."

"I think Dan would say the most beautiful bride was the one last weekend."

"We'll call it a draw. Oh, let me get into my dress," Kay suddenly said, remembering she hadn't changed yet.

Just as Shelby zipped Kay's dress, there was a knock on the door. "That will be your father," Kay said.

"Are you sure he wants to walk me down the aisle? Someone might realize I'm his daughter with a hint like that."

"Sweetheart, today he'll be telling everyone you're his daughter. He's so proud of you."

Shelby drew a deep breath. "Okay, open the door."

Kay swung it open so her husband could see his daughter first thing.

"Oh, Shelby, you're beautiful!"

Shelby laughed. "Your learning curve on the father thing is coming along really well."

He leaned over to kiss her cheek. "So is yours."

Then Dan kissed his wife before sending her out the door.

He turned to Shelby. "You've got to get going. A young man is waiting for you outside," he said.

Taking Shelby's hands in his, he raked his gaze over her, and she could see the pride and affection in his eyes. She started to speak but Dan stopped her.

"There's something I want to tell you, Shelby." He paused a moment, as if searching for the words. "I'm so happy for you and Pete. You're getting the best man I know. He's perfect for my perfect daughter." He swallowed a lump in his throat. "I just want to tell you I love you, Shelby, and I'll spend the rest of my life as close as you want me."

Her eyes sparkling with tears of happiness, she smiled broadly and flung her arms around him. "I love you too…Dad."

At this moment he truly felt like the father she'd yearned for, and he was thrilled she'd chosen now to call him Dad.

He smiled at her. "Now I'm going to lower the front of the veil, if you're ready."

"I am."

The recorded music began just then, and Dan opened the door and proudly led his daughter out to the platform adjacent to the beach.

They headed for Pete, who waited at the end of a temporary aisle formed by the folding chairs. He stood next to the minister in front of a trellis covered with fragrant plumeria.

Shelby kept her eyes on Pete, the man she loved, and all else faded into the background. With a smile on her face and her father at her side, she walked to him, the other half of her soul. She'd traveled four thousand miles to meet him and she didn't intend to put much distance between them for the rest of her life.

She'd never thought of herself as a bride. It was a new role for her. But then, so was daughter to a very handsome father...who married her best "mom."

There had been many surprises in Hawaii.

And she hoped many more little ones to come.

* * * * *

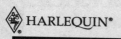

HARLEQUIN®

American ROMANCE®

IS PROUD TO PRESENT A
GUEST APPEARANCE BY

QUILL
BOOK
AWARD
WINNING
AUTHOR

NEW YORK TIMES bestselling author

DEBBIE MACOMBER

The Wyoming Kid

The story of an ex–rodeo cowboy,
a schoolteacher and their journey to the altar.

"Best-selling Macomber, with more than
100 romances and women's fiction titles
to her credit, sure has a way of pleasing readers."
—*Booklist* on *Between Friends*

***The Wyoming Kid* is available from
Harlequin American Romance in July 2006.**

If you enjoyed what you just read,
then we've got an offer you can't resist!

Take 2 bestselling love stories FREE!

Plus get a FREE surprise gift!

Clip this page and mail it to Harlequin Reader Service®

IN U.S.A.
3010 Walden Ave.
P.O. Box 1867
Buffalo, N.Y. 14240-1867

IN CANADA
P.O. Box 609
Fort Erie, Ontario
L2A 5X3

YES! Please send me 2 free Harlequin Romance® novels and my free surprise gift. After receiving them, if I don't wish to receive anymore, I can return the shipping statement marked cancel. If I don't cancel, I will receive 6 brand-new novels every month, before they're available in stores! In the U.S.A., bill me at the bargain price of $3.57 plus 25¢ shipping & handling per book and applicable sales tax, if any*. In Canada, bill me at the bargain price of $4.05 plus 25¢ shipping & handling per book and applicable taxes**. That's the complete price and a savings of 10% off the cover prices—what a great deal! I understand that accepting the 2 free books and gift places me under no obligation ever to buy any books. I can always return a shipment and cancel at any time. Even if I never buy another book from Harlequin, the 2 free books and gift are mine to keep forever.

186 HDN DZ72
386 HDN DZ73

Name	(PLEASE PRINT)	
Address	Apt.#	
City	State/Prov.	Zip/Postal Code

Not valid to current Harlequin Romance® subscribers.
Want to try another series? Call 1-800-873-8635
or visit www.morefreebooks.com.

* Terms and prices subject to change without notice. Sales tax applicable in N.Y.
** Canadian residents will be charged applicable provincial taxes and GST.
   All orders subject to approval. Offer limited to one per household.
   ® are registered trademarks owned and used by the trademark owner and or its licensee.

HROM04R   ©2004 Harlequin Enterprises Limited

Page-turning drama...

Exotic, glamorous locations...

Intense emotion and passionate seduction...

Sheikhs, princes and billionaire tycoons...

This summer, may we suggest:

**THE SHEIKH'S
DISOBEDIENT BRIDE**

by Jane Porter

On sale June.

**AT THE GREEK TYCOON'S
BIDDING**

by Cathy Williams

On sale July.

**THE ITALIAN MILLIONAIRE'S
VIRGIN WIFE**

On sale August.

With new titles to choose from every month,
discover a world of romance in our books written
by internationally bestselling authors.

It's the ultimate in quality romance!

Available wherever Harlequin books are sold.

www.eHarlequin.com   HPGEN06

If you enjoyed what you just read,
then we've got an offer you can't resist!

Take 2 bestselling
love stories FREE!
Plus get a FREE surprise gift!

Clip this page and mail it to Silhouette Reader Service™

IN U.S.A.
3010 Walden Ave.
P.O. Box 1867
Buffalo, N.Y. 14240-1867

IN CANADA
P.O. Box 609
Fort Erie, Ontario
L2A 5X3

YES! Please send me 2 free Silhouette Romance® novels and my free surprise gift. After receiving them, if I don't wish to receive anymore, I can return the shipping statement marked cancel. If I don't cancel, I will receive 4 brand-new novels every month, before they're available in stores! In the U.S.A., bill me at the bargain price of $3.57 plus 25¢ shipping and handling per book and applicable sales tax, if any*. In Canada, bill me at the bargain price of $4.05 plus 25¢ shipping and handling per book and applicable taxes**. That's the complete price and a savings of at least 10% off the cover prices—what a great deal! I understand that accepting the 2 free books and gift places me under no obligation ever to buy any books. I can always return a shipment and cancel at any time. Even if I never buy another book from Silhouette, the 2 free books and gift are mine to keep forever.

210 SDN DZ7L
310 SDN DZ7M

Name	(PLEASE PRINT)	
Address	Apt.#	
City	State/Prov.	Zip/Postal Code

Not valid to current Silhouette Romance® subscribers.

Want to try two free books from another series?
Call 1-800-873-8635 or visit www.morefreebooks.com.

* Terms and prices subject to change without notice. Sales tax applicable in N.Y.
** Canadian residents will be charged applicable provincial taxes and GST.
  All orders subject to approval. Offer limited to one per household.
  ® are registered trademarks owned and used by the trademark owner and or its licensee.

SROM04R   ©2004 Harlequin Enterprises Limited

**Hidden in the secrets of antiquity,
lies the unimagined truth...**

Introducing

ROGUE
Angel™

a brand-new line filled with mystery
and suspense, action and adventure,
and a fascinating look into history.

And it all begins with DESTINY.

In a sealed crypt in
France, where the
terrifying legend of
the beast of Gevaudan
begins to unravel,
Annja Creed discovers
a stunning artifact
that will seal her destiny.

*Available every other
month starting
July 2006, wherever
you buy books.*

GRA1

HOTEL MARCHAND

Four sisters.
A family legacy.
And someone is out to destroy it.

A captivating new limited continuity, launching June 2006

The most beautiful hotel in New Orleans,
and someone is out to destroy it. But mystery,
danger and some surprising family revelations
and discoveries won't stop the Marchand sisters
from protecting their birthright…
and finding love along the way.

HMCD0606

HOTEL MARCHAND

SPECIAL PRICE!

This riveting new saga begins with

In the Dark

by national bestselling author

JUDITH ARNOLD

The party at Hotel Marchand is in full swing when the lights suddenly go out. What does head of security Mac Jensen do first? He's torn between two jobs—protecting the guests at the hotel and keeping the woman he loves safe.

A woman to protect. A hotel to secure. And no idea who's determined to harm them.

On Sale June 2006

SILHOUETTE *Romance*®

COMING NEXT MONTH

#1826 COMING HOME TO THE COWBOY—Patricia Thayer
The Brides of Bella Lucia
Rebecca Valentine might be thriving in the cutthroat world of
New York advertising, but she's losing the battle with her biological
clock. Then her latest assignment takes her to Mitchell Tucker's
ranch. With the cowboy's gentle nudging, Rebecca begins to see
a way to have it all....

#1827 WITH THIS KISS—Susan Meier
The Cupid Campaign
When Rayne Fegan's dad runs afoul of a loan shark and disappears,
she turns to the only man who can help her—her father's nemesis,
Officer Jericho Capriotti. But as their search brings them together,
will their family's feud stand in the way of her happiness?

#1828 NANNY AND THE BEAST—Donna Clayton
The Beast had defeated three of her firm's nannies when owner
Sophia Stanton stepped in to teach him a lesson. Sophia learns
quickly that when Michael Taylor shows fangs, he's really covering
deep wounds. And it isn't long before Sophia realizes that maybe she
is trying too hard to avoid a situation that could be a beauty
with this Beast....

#1829 THE HOMETOWN HERO RETURNS—
Julianna Morris
Luke McCade was gorgeous...*and* the last person Nicki Johansson
wanted to see. No longer the awkward girl from whom he could
steal kisses, Nicki had matured into a gorgeous woman. But could
Luke let go of the past to find a future with her?

SRCNM0706